The Tommy Two Shoes Mysteries

From Mountains to More

Thomas Beck (signature)

Thomas Beck

Laurel Highlands Publishing

The Tommy Two Shoes Mysteries: From mountains to more
Copyright © 2014 Thomas Beck
Rights reserved.

Cover by JosDCreations
http://JosDCreations.com

Laurel Highlands Publishing
Mount Pleasant, PA
USA

http://LaurelHighlandsPublishing.com

ISBN-13: 978-1-941087-07-7
ISBN-10: 1941087078

No part of this book may be reproduced or transmitted in any form or by any means, electronic or mechanical, including photocopying, recording, or by any information storage and retrieval system without the written permission of the author or publisher, except where permitted by law.

This book is a work of fiction. Names, characters, places, and incidents either are products of the author's imagination or are used fictitiously. Any resemblance to actual persons, living or dead, events, or locales is entirely coincidental.

In memory of:
My wife, Cindy
My mother, Sybil
My father, Carl

Table of Contents

Mystery Writer's Mountain Retreat	1
Hey Copper	17
A Soft Spot for Redheads	30
Crime Hits Home	54
Burden of Love	73
Missing	98
More or Les	136
About the Author	162

Mystery Writer's Mountain Retreat

I felt a deep desire to scribble mystery stories for most of my life, but my first adventure into the world of writing didn't happen until after I had retired. Until recently, my only writing was to complete police reports on crimes I'd investigated over the thirty-four years as Pittsburgh police detective. I was about to attend my first retreat for writers. I'd been solving mysteries for a long time and now I wanted to put them on paper for others to read. My creative juices had been bottled up for way too long. I was taking the first step.

The daily grind of logging reports for the police files limited my time for writing and what I could include in my statements as a cop. Now, I was free to explore my creativity and had plans to write about some of my many experiences of crimes I'd solved from memories and my notebooks.

Fate directed me to a small advertisement for the *Wilderness Lodge* describing a retreat for writers in the Pittsburgh Press. I made the decision to start, by registering for the mystery writer's seminar at a resort tucked in the mountains near Denver, Colorado. The flight from Pittsburgh had been uneventful, but tiring. The rolling scenery form the plane's window impressed me with

1

its ever changing beauty. The awe only increased when I saw the mountains as the plane approached the Denver airport.

I almost hoped that Aidan had stayed back in Pittsburgh.

Aidan LeClerc is my partner in crime… solving. While he was alive, he worked as a police reporter. Somehow, he managed to survive from day to day dealing with his multiple phobias. His ghostly being decided to move in with me, and now, I had to live with them. One of his fears was a fear of flying. I had terrible time convincing him that I was heading to Colorado with or without him. If he wanted to travel with me, he'd have to fly.

Late at night to relax after a hard day on the force, I'd fall asleep listening to Aidan share ideas and clues to the case on which I was working. In time, I relied on his help and he attached himself to me.

A moss green van, marked with a gold hued logo and the name of the *Wilderness Lodge,* picked me up at the airport. I was hoping to relax for an hour in my room or somewhere else at the lodge until the evening meal. A younger woman greeted me as I stepped into the wide lobby. "I'm Marsha. Welcome to the *Wilderness Lodge.* How can I help you?"

The highly polished reception desk reflected the softly flickering flames from the lodge's massive, gray stone fireplace. The desk was centered directly beneath the multi-antlered elk chandelier. It was where Marsha Fontaine welcomed me and other guests as they arrived and issued keys to their rooms or cabins.

Marsha was a slender, fretful looking, Caucasian female: five-five, one hundred and five pounds with gray eyes, mousy brown hair and a receding chin. As a cop, I got into the habit of labeling people by their physical attributes. It came in handy when I questioned victims or chased a perpetrator or suspect of a crime as a detective. I had a memory for stats and could readily transfer my observations onto paper when I needed them to write my police report.

I gave her my name, but before she could say more, a ten year old tornado banged open the front door, grabbed an umbrella from a huge copper kettle stand, poked Marsha with the pointed end, then ran up the oak stairway. He disappeared into the second floor, the umbrella left swinging on an antlered light sconce.

"That's my brother, Michael. He can be so hyperactive at times," she apologized. Almost simultaneously, a shapely pair of legs descended the stairs. They belonged to the owner of the lodge, who was Marsha's mother. The woman lifted the still swinging umbrella from the sconce, then replaced it in the urn before entering the dining room.

Marsha handed me the key and a map of the grounds with my cabin circled. She advised me, "We are above eight thousand feet here. You may develop a slight headache and become out of breath more easily. Take your time and you should be fine."

I left the lodge, heading to my cabin. When I dropped my luggage inside my room, I was a little out of breath. I waited a few minutes, before heading back to the deck lined with Adirondack chairs. I wanted to enjoy the serenity until it was time for the evening meal.

※

Wait staff bustled, serving our meal in the cedar-board ceiled dining room. Thick log beams arched high overhead. The centers of the oak tables were made more rustic with small, bright green ferns in copper hued pots.

I'd just finished a wonderfully prepared evening meal of a fresh green salad, a Cornish game hen, and a medley of potatoes and vegetables, but the dessert of peach cobbler topped with a large dollop of whipped cream and the cup of strong, black coffee gave the perfect crowning touch to the meal. The great food and the unobstructed panorama was a wonderful way for me to unwind.

Settling back into my seat, I had the perfect view through the floor to ceiling windows, which overlooked a small lake. Dark spruce and hemlock trees crowded the far shore. In the distance, mountains still retained their crowns of bright snow and ice.

Hearing a cry of, "Oh no!" I tossed my thick linen napkin onto the dining table. Instinctively, I followed the loud cry of distress.

I lumbered into the lobby of the lodge like an old fire horse answering the bell.

Marsha was on her knees, frantically searching for something. As I approached, she muttered, "I have to find my gold pen." She continued to whine, mumbling to herself. "It was my favorite. Lawrence gave that pen to me. I've been writing all of my letters to him with it. I'm sure that he will know it's not the same pen. How will I tell him that I lost it?"

I re-introduced myself to the nearly hysterical girl. "I'm Tommy Two Shoes, can I help?"

I can hear the snickers. Tommy Two Shoes is my nickname. I picked it up after my pop was killed in a Pittsburgh steel mill accident. A heavy roll of steel broke loose, crushing him and injuring several co-workers. My father's death tore my mother's heart out. She never recovered or remarried.

I met many relatives at my dad's funeral, even though I was too young to remember. Aunts, uncles, and cousins flowed in a seemingly endless stream. The one person I remembered the most was my mom's brother, Aidan. Three years later, he lived with us for a short while to support my mom when my brother, John, disappeared from our yard while we were playing. Uncle Aidan and I formed a bond that extended after his passing. He was the person who encouraged me to write.

Like countless others who lost the bread winners in their

family, we had to move in with Nana and Pappy. Nana used to tell us that it was almost as bad for us then as it was for her and Pappy living through the Great Depression.

Mom struggled to keep us fed. There was little money left over for clothing or anything else. To help, I sold newspapers for extra money. That left me almost no time to write.

One year, I had to wear a mismatched pair of shoes to school. Kids could be so cruel. That's how I got the handle of Two Shoes.

I am thankful though. Another boy I knew had to wear a shoe on one foot and a boot on the other. They called him Shoe-Booty.

"I left my pen on the desk when we were called to the dining room and now it's gone! I can't find it anywhere," Marsha's nasal voice keened.

I strolled closer to the reception desk. On top of the mahogany desk was a thin sheaf of sea foam green paper. The top page had writing on it. Marsha popped up and quickly turned the page over. It was as if she were afraid that I would read what she had been writing to Lawrence. The polished, dark desk softly reflected the glow of the crackling flames from the fireplace.

As other diners finished their meals, they slowly drifted into the lobby, drawn by the noise and activity. The would-be mystery writers reluctantly began to help look for the missing pen. One by one, they joined the search party, just to quiet Marsha's mewling voice. Many of the hunters ended their search patterns back in their own rooms or cabins.

Marie Fontaine was a small boned, Caucasian female: five four, about one hundred fifteen, cornflower blue eyes, thin lips, prematurely silver hair, and approximately fifty-six. After making her own search, she said, "Marsha, we will look again in the morning."

Marie called, "Louisa, come here please." Louisa's thickly

soled shoes padded softly across the lodge-pine floor. She wore a gold badge with her name etched on it, pinned to the left shoulder of her pale blue uniform.

"Yes, ma'am."

"When you clean later today, I want you to pay special attention to the lobby. Marsha has lost her gold fountain pen. I would like you to look for it."

"Yes, ma'am."

I noticed that Louisa didn't look at Marie as Marie spoke to her. She continued to look down at the laces on her shoes. Only the top of her black hair pulled back into a tight bun was visible. From my past experiences, people who were less than honest always refused to look me in the eye.

Marie didn't say more, and Louisa hurried back down a hallway.

※

The cabin I'd been assigned was about one hundred yards from the main lodge. It was a small cedar clapped building with patches of moss growing on its shake roof. The wood had weathered to a dark coffee brown color. A screened door protected the wide plank door from bugs and allowed for the circulation of air if I chose not to use the window air conditioner. I was unsure if Aidan had followed me to Colorado, until he saw that I had chosen a plain, rustic, outside cabin and not one of the rooms inside of the main lodge. He tended to appear with scents of cleaning supplies. I smelled chlorine bleach. We had a royal fight and the smell increased to assault me.

"*I am not sleeping in there. There has to be spiders, bugs, snakes and rats. Cabins are nasty things. You can't be serious about me staying in there for the weekend. I can't stand dust and spider webs.*"

I was unsure whether Uncle Aidan was passing a clue to me in his usual oblique way or whether he was just grousing about my choice.

Unlocking the door, I could tell by the increasing smell of chlorine bleach that my uncle was peering over my shoulder, scrutinizing the inside of the room. *Look, Uncle Aidan, it's clean. There's no dust, no spider webs, and no snakes. This place is already filled with the aroma of Pine-Sol. That should make you feel right at home. Even the bed linens are clean and smell freshly washed. If you don't like the cabin and don't think it's clean enough for you, you can climb a tree and spend the night in a squirrel's nest for all I care.*

I won't repeat what my uncle answered.

※

It must have been the freshness of the mountain air that woke me so early. I looked out onto the small lake in front of my cabin in time to see the view just before the sun rose. Thin wisps of fog embroidered intricate patterns over the surface of the water. I stepped outside of my cabin onto the tiny, cedar stoop. The atmosphere was thin at that altitude, but the air tasted fresh and delicious.

As I stood on the postage-stamp porch, a fish rose to disturb the smooth surface of the lake and vanished with a swirl. In the distance, a bull elk bugled. The echo resounded over the placid water from a dark stand of pines on the far shore. The sum of it all was so overwhelmingly beautiful, that it actually brought a lump to my throat. Even a hardened Pittsburgh cop could be touched by the beauty of nature.

I hiked back to the lodge along the narrow, stone pathway. The lawn sloped down from the left to the lake. A low rock wall was the only railing to my right. Thick plantings of ivy covered the top of the wall, draping down over the sides. Limbs from cedar and pine trees kept the walkway cool and shaded for most of the day. The lights of the lodge drew me like a moth to a flame.

Hungry, I thought I'd see if they were serving breakfast yet or at least get a cup of coffee. When I entered the lodge, I heard a distinctly French accented voice spill out of the kitchen, saying, "*Mon Dieu*, where is my meat thermometer? I cannot roast this venison haunch for lunch without it. It was here with the roasting pan when I went to bed last night. Marie, I cannot disappoint our guests."

Marie's soothing voice cooed, "*Mon Cheri*, it will be all right. You are a great chef. You don't need the thermometer to prepare the roast perfectly. I have been at your side for nearly twenty-five years. You've never served a bad meal. In all of my life, you've never let me down." I could hear them murmur for a few seconds more and then the buss of a kiss before Marie emerged from the galley.

"Good morning," she greeted. "I hope you slept well."

"I did and good morning to you."

"If you are you ready for breakfast, I would highly recommend the blueberry pancakes. They are very light and fluffy. My husband, François, has outdone himself this morning."

I agreed with her suggestion and ordered a cup of coffee as well. The coffee was hot, dark and rich. Exactly the way I liked it.

I had only taken a few sips when Marie returned with my pancakes. There were only four of them, but the stack was nearly six inches high. A large spoonful of blueberries had been placed on the top of the steaming pancakes. Butter oozed from between each flapjack while two pats still melted on top. Marie placed a small jug of syrup on the table as well.

If the rest of the retreat and the food was as good as the meal I'd already had, I was in for a real treat. It looked so much better than anything I ever made for breakfast at home.

Cutting through the stack without spilling the blueberries

down the side was quite a task. As I lifted the first bite, I could smell pine and it wasn't coming from outside. It was Pine-Sol. Uncle Aidan had returned. I looked around the dining room to see if he had entered the room as a visible wisp or just a voice in my ear.

That was all that I needed. *Aidan, you're coming between me and my breakfast. I was just getting used to your antiseptic smell interrupting me, but this is too much. I came here to smell real pine and real food, not Pine-Sol.* I interrupted before he could speak. *Can't I just once enjoy my meal without the odor of your Pine-Sol spoiling it all?*

Unfortunately, that didn't deter him and he pressed on. "I just came to warn you to be careful with those blueberries. They'll stain your clothing and you may not find something that will remove it."

I know what people may think, a ghost as my partner, right? I just consider him as an inner voice. I finally opened my mind to his continued prodding as he identified himself as my kin and a friend with odd compulsions. Our initial encounter was sudden. I didn't recognize what it was at first. I smelled bleach mixed with the odor of cleaning supplies. It wrapped around me like a thick, smothering blanket. I was younger then and didn't recognize who it was that was talking when Uncle Aidan started to speak to me. It was our very first meeting after he passed away. As I struggled with a case that was lengthy, confusing, and complicated, Aidan slipped me the key that unlocked the answer. It was the beginning of our partnership and he has fed me clues ever since.

Uncle LeClerc was a neat-freak while living with us. When I understood that it was to be an ongoing relationship, I said, *Uncle LeClerc? You're going to be my partner? I can't believe I'd get stuck with someone who uses as many cleaning supplies as you do.*

"*I know what you're thinking,*" Aidan replied, "*but I'm not completely thrilled with this arrangement either. I was assigned to you, although you were my favorite nephew. Someone on the other side must want you to be more careful and NEAT."*

I can't understand why I have to be partnered with you?

"I may be just a little neurotic about cleanliness, but I can give you fresh insight, if nothing else. My work skills makes me a perfect partner. You're old and stodgy and have a one track mind. You're used to working with a partner and heaven knows now that you've retired, you're going to need help. I can offer it.

"Remember, I worked as a reporter for a police newspaper. I wrote about crime solving with nothing more than smells, an offhand word, a scrap of paper, or a single thread from a piece of fabric. I had to keep track of all sorts of details. And now, I'm able to foresee some things even before they happen. What do you think of that? Am I the right person for the job?"

All right, all right. You win, Uncle Aidan. I guess I do need a partner now that I've retired, even if it is you.

※

Clyde was another mystery writer at our conference. I became acquainted with him when he entered the dining area after finding some of his property missing. He was searching for Marie. Spying her at my table, he walked across the room keeping a hand in front of his mouth.

Since the dining room was empty, I had invited Marie to sit with me until her other guests arrived. She daintily sipped a cup of Chamomile tea, when Clyde, a male Caucasian, late thirties, average height and weight, brown hair and eyes, walked up to our table. "Did someone come into my room last night?" he asked Marie. His room was in the lodge itself.

"Certainly not," Marie replied. She seemed a bit offended by the question, thinking that he suggested that one of her staff had accessed his room during the night.

Talking with his hand still covering his mouth, Clyde said,

"Someone must have been in my room. My partial plate with gold teeth on it is missing. I have been searching for nearly an hour and I can't find it."

"Let me help you look," Marie offered, replacing her cup on the saucer. Being the curious ex-cop that I was, I trailed close on their heels. We climbed the oak staircase. Antlers that had been converted to shade-covered sconces festooned the wall and lighted our way up the split log treads.

Clyde's room was disheveled. Clothes were tossed about everywhere. "Sorry about the mess, but I have gone through absolutely everything and my partial plate is not here." His hand still muted his voice.

I asked, "Where was the last place you had it?"

"If you find it, don't touch it. After all, it was in his mouth," Aidan warned as a puff of Lysol wafted past me. *"There has to be germs on it."*

"It was there on the nightstand, beside the lamp."

Although I was sure that he had already moved the lamp and the nightstand, I shifted them just the same, double checking. Marie was on her hands and knees, groping blindly beneath the beds. She came up with nothing for all of her effort, not even a dust-bunny. Even after shaking out the bed linens and refolding Clyde's clothing, her search was unfruitful.

"I will tell Louisa to keep a sharp eye out for your missing denture. I am sure she will find it," she promised. "I'll have breakfast served in your room if you wish. Tell me what you would like to eat."

Obviously upset, he growled, "What I'd like to eat and what I'll be able to eat are two different things. I don't have my teeth to chew on anything. Send a bowl of oatmeal."

Earlier, I thought the missing items might be a vendetta against the Fontaine's and the inn. However, Clyde's stolen denture put a whole new perspective on the missing items. I began to think that Michael might have taken and misplaced the missing items. Why would anyone steal them? The belongings weren't very valuable.

I went back to my table to have a second cup of coffee and studied the other writers as they filtered in for breakfast.

The rising sun had long since burned off the fog. The mirror-like lake reflected the sun's rays through the tall windows of the lodge. Marie slid the sheer curtains over the wide expanse of glass to cut the blinding glare that poured into the room, but it still allowed a magnificent view of the lake outdoors and the mountains beyond. The vast panorama, which was beautiful before, took on an ethereal quality. I've never been considered a sensitive cop, but I could never find a view like this in Pittsburgh, even on Mount Washington.

A late comer entered the dining room. A female Caucasian, five six, two hundred pounds, deep set brown eyes, bleach blond hair, and tortoise-shell glasses stood at the door. She had a worried look on her face. "I am missing my gold pin," she blurted out to no one and yet to everyone present. Her pale hand pressed against her chest where I'd seen her gold, rose-shaped brooch pinned the night before.

Marie stood. I watched her cross the room to join the newly distressed guest. Marie's curled hair bounced, shaking her head in disbelief as she heard the news. I knew she had to be thinking, "Oh no. Not again. Not another one."

After hurrying to the distraught woman's side, Marie said, "Let's go back to your room and see what we can find, Norma." Marie escorted the newest victim back to the guest's cabin to search for the missing piece of jewelry. I didn't follow. I was sure that they wouldn't be able to find the pin either. Someone here was a brazen thief, confident enough to steal four items, one after another. The criminal was somewhere in the lodge. Marie had to be worried about the reputation of her lodge.

Knowing that I was the only cop present, I felt it was in some way my duty to solve the mystery of the missing items. I chose to be a cop because the police failed to find my brother, John, when he went missing from our Munhall home. I had been solving other people's mysteries ever since.

The thefts had to stop. The safety and good standing of Marie's inn was at stake.

The perfume of chlorine bleach preceded Aidan's arrival. His ghost never actually made a physical appearance, but merely whispered in my ear. *"You're close, but you're not quite right, Tommy. You're outside of your comfort zone."*

When Marie came back into the dining area, she had a distressed look on her face. She was talking to a lanky, bald man. He was nattily dressed with a polka-dotted bow tie. His gray eyes gave furtive glances and his hands moved restlessly. In general, his appearance somehow seemed shiftless to me.

"You'll end up having to watch him. He may just teach you something," Aidan said.

※

The writers met in the dining area after the tables had been cleared for the morning lecture. I sat in a corner where I could watch all of the other writers. Clyde was the only writer missing. Surely, he was embarrassed about the gap in his smile. I eliminated him as a suspect. He, too, was a victim.

When the speaker walked to the lectern, it was the lanky, bald man who I'd seen with Marie earlier. She introduced the man, "This is Mr. Melchior. He's the speaker for our symposium and the author of several best-selling detective and mystery books. He's taught writing at Pietown University for seventeen years." Marie walked away.

When I saw that the bald man was the speaker, I knew Uncle

Aidan was laughing. *Very funny, I should have known that when your clue seemed too straight forward, you were just jerking me around.*

Then I thought, *Perhaps Mr. Melchior was taking the items to see if any of the attendees were observant enough to catch him in the act.* I'd still need to keep an eye on him.

While listening to the speaker, subtly Uncle LeClerc started to intrude on my thoughts. The aroma of Lysol drifted in. I had a mental image that Aidan was trying to tell me something, but he wasn't speaking loudly enough to be clear. Why wasn't I hearing him? I was unsure of what he said.

What are you trying to tell me? Talk louder. I can't understand you.

Because I couldn't understand, Aidan became frustrated and finally yelled, "*Rats!*" before disappearing.

After Aidan left, I listened to Melchior speak about the usual methods that professional sleuths used to set traps for criminals and then how to do surveillance on the bait. Surveillance was something that I had done many times over the years. I have the calluses on my keister to prove it. I also have a ten gallon bladder from swilling coffee to keep awake without having a bathroom nearby.

That's what I'll do. I snapped my fingers, deciding that's exactly what I'd do. I'd set a trap. The first item disappeared from the desk top. So, I placed my silver money clip on the desk. That would be the bait. It was devoid of any cash. My clip would be in a spot where it would be easy for Mr. Melchior, Louisa, or Michael to pick it up.

I pulled a chair from the lecture area to an area where I could surreptitiously watch the registration desk with my money clip, the writers sitting for the lecture, and the comings and goings of any of the attendees in the dining room. My eyelids began to droop and my head nodded as I listened to the monotone droning of the speaker extolling the virtues of the stake out.

Aidan whispered loudly in my ear, *"Don't fall asleep now."*

Mystery Writer's Mountain Retreat

The odor of Lysol filled the air and I sneezed. I certainly couldn't nod off again, not with that smell in my face. Aidan had disappeared, but the cloying odor of Lysol clung to my nostrils.

I noticed a slight movement near the desk. It was small, furtive, and furry. I sat bolt upright. What was that? Had I actually fallen asleep? Was I dreaming?

Instantly, I was on alert and ready for action when a creature hopped onto the chair's seat, then up onto the desktop. The rodent-like animal picked up my money clip in its mouth, then leaped down from the desk. I bounded out of the chair and chased it. I wasn't about to lose the clip I'd gotten as a retirement gift.

It scooted outside through a crack between the double screened doors, then hurried down the rocky terrace. The creature dove headlong into a stack of cut-firewood. Following it, I tossed the chunks of wood aside. The missing items were cradled in a nest of leaves and grass.

I fetched the fetching Mrs. Fontaine outside, leading her to the uncovered lair in the woodpile. I showed her what I had found.

"It's not an actual thief, just a pack rat. I am so relieved. The good name of my lodge has been saved. Thank you so very much," Marie said, beaming. "I'll seal all off the cracks once your group departs and set traps."

We gathered the items from the nest and returned them to their rightful owners. *Yes, Aidan, I allowed Marie to carry the denture.*

At least the seminar wasn't a total waste, I'd learned something. I had misread Louisa's reluctance to look into Marie's eyes as guilt, when it was cultural. She'd been raised to believe that looking into the eyes of the boss was disrespectful.

Clyde joined the group of writers, after his denture had a good brushing, I am sure. The gold fountain pen was back in

Marsha's possession. Clasping it to her breast, her eyes filled with tears. Norma got her gold rose pin back and François had his thermometer returned. By the way, François, the venison was succulent and delicious.

I was pocketing my money clip when Aidan LeClerc reminded, *"I gave you all the clues. What took you so long? If we continue to be partners, you're going to have to pay more attention to what I say."*

I said, You win, Aidan. The next time we have to travel, I'll pack extra hand sanitizer, if that okay with you? He didn't reply, but I just knew he was smiling.

Hey Copper

Achoo. I sneezed, waking myself out of a sound sleep.

"Are you sleeping?" Aidan asked.

The stringent odors of cleaning fluids and chlorine bleach filled my nostrils and my bedroom. Immediately, my eyes popped open. "Not now," I replied testily. I became used to my uncle, Aidan LeClerc, "talking" to me, but not in the middle of the night. I got familiar with the ghost of my deceased uncle being my partner, but not until I had almost retired from the City of Pittsburgh Bureau of Police. After thirty four years, I was done with investigating murders, druggies, and assaults. I wanted something safer and a little stressful.

Before I retired, I would sit in my recliner and watch television when I was off-shift. It helped me to unwind from the stress of police work. After I fell asleep, Uncle Aidan would visit me, reviewing the clues and sharing insight to the case that I was working. He had been a police reporter. Though it sounds odd, his ghostly review of my cases often gave me the advice I needed to solve them. His directions were correct. He slowly evolved from visiting me in my dreams, to the point he would arrive at any time, cloaked in the smell of cleaning supplies.

When I first retired, I spent many restless nights, sleeping lightly. Constantly, I was on the alert, waiting for the phone to wake me with a new crime to investigate. Eventually, I got comfortable sleeping the whole night through without interruption and now Uncle Aidan intruded on my rest, stinking up my bedroom. Of all the helpers in the world, I got stuck with an overly clean person like Aidan LeClerc. I'm sure he would say the same thing about me, but just the reverse—I'm sloppy. We were almost like Tony Randal and Jack Klugman on the T.V. series *the Odd Couple*.

Since his death, the one great joy of Aidan's "life" was intruding into my mind and into my life. He'd complain about how messy I was. He frequently shared his know-how to "help" me solve the mysteries that I found, but the information was so infinitely subtle and vague they always seemed obscure. Only after piecing together a long list of his clues, could I actually see and follow a thread that would help me solve the crime.

I had similar problems with my ex-wife. She would wake me after I had spent most of the night on a call, then giving me a very obscure hint as to what she wanted. That's one of the reasons she's my ex.

I know there are people who will say that a cop or even an ex-cop who talks to a ghost, even if it is an uncle, has gone over the edge, but we all have that inner voice. Mine just happens to be my uncle, Aidan LeClerc.

Startled awake, I couldn't get back to sleep. The lingering odor of cleaning fluids remained in the room even though it did seem to lessen somewhat after Aidan disappeared.

At one time, the ticking of my battered wind-up alarm clock lulled me to sleep, but tonight, it assaulted me as it rested on the cheap, wood grained table beside my head. I glanced at its dark face. With the streetlight filtering through my window, shining on the luminescent hands, I could see it was nearly two a. m.

Why in the world would you wake me, Aidan? I was so upset. I wanted to punch something. I rolled onto my side and slugged my pillow several times, trying to get comfortable again.

I had almost dozed off when the loud sound of shattering glass and a piercing scream echoed in my ears. Bolting upright in my bed, I automatically grabbed the snub-nosed 38 that I kept tucked under my pillow. I struggled into my pants, having only one hand free. With my slippers flapping, I raced from my apartment. The sounds came from the apartment directly below mine.

Yanking open the door to the fire stairway, I pounded my way down the steps. My feet hitting the metal stairs in the enclosed staircase made my ears ring. I slipped the safety off my revolver, as I exited the stairwell.

I rapped on the door. "Mrs. McMurtry. It's Tommy Two Shoes from the apartment upstairs. Are you okay?"

A shuffling gait softly scuffed to the door. The dead bolt turned and the door opened a crack, as far as the safety chain would allow. Her pale, frightened face appeared in the narrow opening. "Thank God it's you, Tommy." She closed the door. I thought at first she was dismissing me, until I heard the chain being unfastened.

The door reopened. She said in a shaky voice barely above a whisper, "Come in."

The cop in me responded, "What happened?"

"Someone tried to break into my bedroom until I screamed and threw a shoe at him."

Moving past her, I saw an old, wooden baseball bat lying on her sofa. I smiled, knowing that she wasn't completely helpless. Carefully, I slipped through her living room with my gun in hand, then stepped into her darkened bedroom, allowing my pistol to precede me. The apartments were laid-out much the same and I flipped on the light switch without taking my eyes off the interior of the room. The bottom pane of the window had been shattered. Shards of glass were strewn across her worn linoleum floor and onto the thick throw rug at her bedside. When I scanned the crime scene, it seemed empty. Only the bathroom and a closet needed to be cleared before I would feel safe and comfortable. My quick inspection revealed nothing. I looked out onto the concrete sidewalk just to be sure and there was Mrs. McMurtry's black tie-up shoe.

"*Aren't you going to clean up the glass?*" Aidan pressed. "*It's dangerous.*" The smells of the city had almost obscured the odor of Spic 'N Span.

Aidan, you've reported on crime scenes before. You know I can't touch anything until the investigating officers are through.

"*I know, but it's just so messy.*"

"All clear," I said to Mrs. McMurtry. I could hear the approaching wail of a siren pour through the window's new opening. Tucking my revolver into my waistband behind my back, I waited. I had no desire to meet two policemen answering a break-in call with a gun in my fist.

When they arrived, I greeted them, "Marty. Dave. Glad to see you guys. It's been awhile."

Both officers had their hands hovering over their holstered weapons.

"Tommy, what are you doing here? I thought you retired," Marty said.

"I did, but I live upstairs. When I heard Mrs. McMurtry scream, I came running. Like an old fighter coming out at the bell, I guess. I did a quick sweep of the place. The perp isn't here."

Just like I would have done, they made their own thorough search, investigating the entire apartment.

"All clear," they agreed.

I did a synopsis of my involvement before they released me. They still needed to question Mrs. McMurtry and I needed to get back to sleep.

I said, "You have my statement. I'll check with the station tomorrow morning to see if anything else is needed for the report. I'm heading to bed. G'night guys."

As I was drifting off to sleep, I heard Aidan say, "*You've changed, Tommy boy. You've changed. Rolling out of bed in the middle of the night used to not bother you.*" Then silence.

I knew he had just slipped me a clue, but I was too sleepy and decided I would try to deal with that addition to the puzzle in the morning.

※

I felt like I'd been drugged when I woke. *Aidan said I'd been getting soft. He must be right. I once was used to those middle-of-the-night calls and now a little interruption like last night—*

Digging into my cupboards, I began to see what I could scrounge up for breakfast. I found some instant coffee, a half empty jar of peanut butter, and a few slices of bread. Looking into the bread bag, I could see there was some bread inside, but there was mold on the edge of the crusts. I pulled out two of the dry slices, ripped off the moldy parts, and stuck them into the toaster. *What can I say? It was breakfast.*

"*You're not actually going to eat that, are you?*" Aidan nagged.

I'm almost grateful for your Pine-Sol smell this morning, Aidan. There is nothing else in the house to eat, and besides, I'm hungry. If you don't like what I'm eating, run around the corner to the cafe and get breakfast for both of us.

"But it has mold on it."

The cafe or be quiet.

The curious cop part of me kept my brain in motion. I wanted to get my hands on that police report. I showered and took a cab to the station.

As I pulled open the double glass doors, a friendly voice called out, "Hey, Tommy. Long time, no see."

"You old codger, I thought you'd have retired by now," I bantered. "Sergeant Duggan, you haven't changed a bit."

"You still tell lies, Tommy Two Shoes. I did hear you had some action out your way last night."

"It sure was a surprise to me happening in the middle of the night, like that. I came down to be sure my statement was correct." I knew that by asking, I could eye ball the rest of the report to see what other information Dave and Marty had collected. As a civilian, I wouldn't normally be able to see what the investigators had found, but recently retired, I guess it gave me a little leeway.

Glancing up from reading the report, I asked, "Sarge, have there been any home invasions or rapes in my neighborhood?"

"I'm not aware of any, Tommy. There was a rape in the next borough, but the age was way off. She was a much younger woman."

Aidan's voice echoed in my head. *"Well, that's a theory that's out the window."*

I muttered, "Thanks." I groaned at my uncle's heavy handed attempt at a pun.

I must have said it out loud, because Duggan replied, "No problem, Tommy boy, anytime."

As I left the station, I walked into a cloud of Pine-Sol. LeClerc chided, *"You need to be careful talking aloud to me. They'll think you're crazy."*

Back to square one, I thought.

※

When I entered my apartment, I reviewed the facts from the crime report. *Nada.* I got zip from the report that I didn't already know. I added that information and the clues that Aidan gave me to my notebook.

"Nothing makes any sense yet, does it?" Aidan interrupted, shooting me another clue.

Thanks for the help, but don't bother me now. I need to find the common links. After a few minutes of pushing the cards around, I was no closer to seeing the answer.

I knew that answer was there. It just had to be. I needed to give Mrs. McMurtry her peace of mind back.

"You can't make heads or tails of it yet, because you're missing facts," Aidan said.

I looked over my cards and I had to agree.

I think we need to talk with Mrs. McMurtry again, Aidan.

"We have to find out what she did and where she went all last week, Tommy."

I was back to writing down the questions I wanted to ask her. I wanted to hear the answers from her myself. She had to go over everything in detail; each and every thing that she'd done in the past week or so. She had to recall every step that she took.

"That may be the key," Aidan said. The scent of Lysol disappeared.

Uncle Aidan was gone and I was talking to myself.

Lifting the receiver, I dialed Mrs. McMurtry. She answered on the third ring. "Hello?" I could hear the trepidation in her voice. Any person, after a scare like last night, would be concerned with who was calling.

"It's me, Mrs. McMurtry, Tommy Two Shoes. I was wondering if I could ask you a few more questions about last night?"

She hesitated for a second, then said, "If it will make me feel safe again and catch the man who tried to break in, yes. Give me fifteen minutes." Her voice was stronger. A sense of determination had emerged. The woman that kept a bat in her apartment was back.

I knew that the perpetrator was a man from what I'd read in the police report. Mrs. McMurtry described the silhouette she saw at the window by the light of the streetlamps. It was definitely a male.

I could smell coffee as I approached her apartment. Real, fresh-brewed coffee, not the swill I'd made for breakfast. My mouth watered. I could almost taste it as I deeply inhaled its rich deliciousness, then tapped on her door.

The lock turned, the door opened as wide as the security chain would allow. She peered out through the crack before removing the chain. Even though she knew that I was coming, I couldn't blame her for being cautious.

"Have a seat, young man." She indicated a chair with a mug of steaming joe on the table beside it. "I believe you still take it black?"

"Yes, ma'am. You have an excellent memory." She had eaten lunch with us before my wife and I separated.

I pulled out a pad and pen. It felt good having my hands on the tools of my trade and actually using them again doing an interview. "I read the police report this morning. There was nothing of much importance in it. Have you thought of anything else that you didn't tell the officers last night?"

When she shook her head no, Aidan interrupted, *"She hasn't remembered everything. I saw her wrinkle her brow and purse her lips. Ask her to go over all the things she did this week."* Uncle Aidan's voice poured over my head from a Pine-Sol bottle. His appearance smothered the aroma of my coffee, ruining the taste, and that upset me.

Another clue, I surmised, then mentally complained. *Aidan LeClerc, why can't you be less subtle? I'm striking out here. Either say what you mean or back off. I want to be able to enjoy my cup of coffee.*

Strike one.

"Get her to open up," my uncle chided, ignoring my complaint.

I flipped to the back of my note pad and wrote verbatim the clues that Aidan had been sharing. I'd look for the common thread later.

"Mrs. McMurtry, did you stay inside all day yesterday?"

She paused, then said, "I only went to the corner store and bought a quart of milk and a loaf of bread."

Bread, I need to buy a loaf, too, I thought, as I flipped to the notebook's back pages. I started my own grocery list: coffee, bread, eggs.

I walked her back though the week. Other than a few friends dropping in to visit, there was nothing unusual.

Strike two.

※

Back in my apartment, I listed everything I'd learned onto more three by five cards, including Aidan's new hints and Mrs. McMurtry's statements. Adding and shuffling the new facts into different orders, I was hoping that a pattern would emerge. I sat at my Formica topped kitchen table for nearly an hour before I gave up and ducked out to the store before it closed for a few breakfast items: a bag of fresh roasted coffee beans, eggs, milk, and a loaf of whole wheat bread. I gave the clerk a ten spot. He rang the cash register and then said, "Here's your change sir."

When I got back to my apartment, I gave the cards another shot. Sitting at my kitchen table, I stared blankly at the clues. Aidan interrupted in a thick cloud of a germicidal mist, *"A penny for your thoughts."*

I'm coming up blank. I'm not seeing it.

"Are you slipping? You used to be an excellent copper. Have you gone soft since you've retired? Have you actually changed that much?"

His snide comments didn't deserve an answer, but I copied the new clues, if they were clues and not insults being hurled at me, onto a few more index cards and added them to the pile.

I was about to set them aside when a thought hit me. I grabbed his clues, shuffled them, I rearranged them one more time, and looked for the idea of the common thread that popped into my head. There it was. How could I have missed it?

That has to be it, Uncle.

I needed to talk with Mrs. McMurtry again, but looking at my watch, I saw it was too late to bother her tonight. I'd approach her first thing in the morning.

She would be safe in her apartment. Previously, I helped the Super screw the half inch thick plywood over the broken window pane in her bedroom. It looked like a thick wooden eye patch, but it would hold. I'd seen the deadbolt on her door and it would need a battering ram to force it open. I could get a good night's sleep and now that I had groceries, I would have a tasty breakfast if LeClerc would only let me alone.

※

After a hot cup of coffee and a good breakfast, I phoned Mrs. McMurtry. "I have an idea about the break-in. I'd like to ask a few more questions if I could and check out a thought that I had."

There was no hesitation at all in her voice, "Fifteen minutes, Tommy. The coffee will be ready."

Once I settled inside her apartment, I asked, "When you went shopping, did you get any change back from your purchases?"

"Yes, yes I did."

"You haven't spent any of it yet, have you?" I asked.

"I haven't left my apartment since then. I felt a little worn out after all of the excitement."

"May I see the money?"

"Let me get my handbag."

She levered herself out of her lumpy, flowered chair and walked to a small half table in the hallway. She reached inside a well-worn, brown leather handbag and withdrew a large, lumpy change purse. She handed it to me as she sat back down.

The purse was heavy. When I emptied the contents onto her coffee table, I heard a loud clunk.

There it is. That has to be the answer. It has to be that roll of pennies. All of Aidan's clues pointed to those pennies as the motive.

"May I open this?" I asked as I hefted the roll of coins in my hand.

She nodded her assent.

I unfolded the end-flaps of the wrapper. When I dumped the

contents onto the table, I noticed that a name and address had been written on the wrapper's outside. Carefully, I expressed all of the coins, making sure I didn't damage any evidence left on the wrapper. The coins spilled out, ringing on the table's marble surface. I carefully set the paper wrapping with the name aside. If my assumption was correct, the wrapper would be needed as evidence. My eyes lit up as I saw the coins that were spread out on the tabletop.

I was so absorbed with the task at hand, I barely heard Mrs. McMurtry explain how she had gotten the pennies. "The grocer was low on change and asked if I minded taking part of my change in a roll of pennies. I said, 'Not at all.'"

The display of pennies on the table was speaking to me as loudly as she was.

Using a fingernail, I separated the coins. There were a lot of wheat pennies, and several Indian head pennies, but one coin stood out from all the rest. It was a different color from all the others. I nudged it out where I could see it better. It was an 1888 brass Indian head penny, not like the usual copper colored one cent pieces.

"Mrs. McMurtry, this one penny alone is worth between $20,000 and $25,000. After just a quick tally, I'd say you have nearly $40,000 worth of pennies here on your coffee table."

"Oh, my word," she gasped, putting her hand to her mouth.

"I think someone accidentally spent these pennies and wanted them back."

"Goodness gracious," Mrs. McMurtry exclaimed. "All he would have needed was to have asked me and I would have given them back."

"May I use your phone?" When she nodded, I picked up her telephone and dialed the police station. "Hey, Sarge, this is

Tommy Two Shoes. On the break-in case at my apartment complex, did they find any fingerprints?"

"Let me check, Tommy boy."

After a few minutes, the voice returned. "Forensics lifted a finger and partial thumbprint off the stoop railing."

"Can you send some detectives over to Mrs. McMurtry's apartment? I think I found evidence, the motive, and a suspect. Oh, and make sure the detectives pick up some cloth gloves. This evidence will need to be handled with care."

After I hung up, I cautioned her not to touch the pennies. "Handling them without wearing gloves can affect their value."

"Can you wait with me, Tommy?" she asked. "There's still plenty of coffee.

A Soft Spot for Redheads

I love Pittsburgh. Its diversity of people, culture, and architecture made it an interesting place for me to work and live. Some of the views in the city are quite spectacular, but not mine. Mine sucks. Out of my apartment windows, I can see a brick wall with peeling paint and pigeon streaks.

I returned to the neighborhood where I had walked a beat as a rookie for the Pittsburgh Police Department once I called it quits with my wife after twenty years. I was fortunate enough to find a small apartment in my old neighborhood that I could afford on a cop's salary minus the spousal support. I have since retired from the police department after thirty-four years of service.

My apartment suited me when I worked long hours for the city, but now that I'd retired, it felt cramped and I felt confined. I was getting restless. I needed something to do. That and gaining a few pounds got me to think about exercising.

I'd solved a few mysteries since my retirement and knew when I'd smell the subtle and often not so subtle odors of cleaning fluids, it meant the ghost of my uncle Aidan LeClerc and I would soon be on a new case. Uncle LeClerc had been a local police reporter and now he thinks he's my partner.

My gut began to expand and to do a Jell-o jiggle after I retired. Now that I had the time, I decided to get some exercise and become reoriented to the neighborhood simultaneously. I wanted to check out any changes.

When I finished my breakfast, I headed to my favorite living room chair. Sitting down, I put on my shoes. *Chair, don't get too comfortable with me sitting here. I'm going for a walk.*

I pulled on my high-top, black brogans and tied them tightly. *No time like the present to start walking the old beat.* I wanted to get my exercise over and done with before the heat drove me back inside. I was not getting paid to walk the streets in the rain and heat anymore.

After hoofing along for several blocks, I saw a small cafe that I remembered from walking the neighborhood and decided to duck inside. I was on familiar ground and had spent quite a few evenings at the counter enjoying a cup of coffee, resting my feet, or just getting out of the weather, making rounds on my beat as a patrolman.

The faded logo of P's Café was still emblazoned on the thick glass pane of the old wooden door and on the metal placard that spread itself across the front of the building. The brass handles of the door were polished and shining from many years of use.

Pushing the door open, I heard the familiar jingle of the small, silver bells roped to the door handle with a red tasseled cord. As I glanced around, the inside of the place hadn't changed a bit over the many intervening years. Three small tables were arranged along one wall, two red chairs for each of the tables and eight red Naugahyde stools crowded around a curved green Formica countertop. I remembered that the owner, old man Vinnie Polanski, made a mean cup of coffee.

I immediately smelled the odor of the cleaning fluids Aidan usually shared with me. The mystery started here and now. I just knew it.

A flaming expanse of hair rose from behind the counter. When I saw the tall buxom, redhead appear, I was more than pleasantly surprised. *That's a definite change for the better. And that's definitely not old Vinnie Polanski.* It was a Rita Hayward moment from that *Gilda* movie.

I grabbed a stool at the counter. Unfortunately the lumps in the stools hadn't changed. I shifted my position to get more comfortable, if a person can get comfortable on one of those stools. The ginger-haired beauty grabbed a menu and sauntered over. "Hi. What can I get for you?"

She was five-eight, one hundred-twenty-five pounds with startling green eyes and a smattering of freckles across her nose. Her bright red lips widened into an enchanting smile revealing almost perfect white teeth.

"I'll have a cup of coffee, if you make it as hot, strong, and black as old man Polanski did."

She swayed away from the spot where I was sitting, grabbed a cup from beneath the counter then, lifted the pot of coffee to pour. "So you knew my granddad?" she called over her shoulder.

"Yeah, I knew Vinnie."

I was enjoying the view now that it had been exposed without the intervening curtain of apron in the way. The slim waist and the fullness of her hips were accentuated by her tight, faded jeans she was wearing.

I'll have to stop in here more often.

"My name's Tommy Two Shoes," I said, introducing myself.

She didn't bat an eye at the mention of my nickname, but then a lot of guys in this neighborhood still used nicknames.

She placed the steaming cup of coffee on the counter, slid a spoon beside it, and nudged a small creamer closer, before proffering a smooth hand with bright red finger nails to me. "I'm Vera Polanski. Vinnie passed away several years ago and I inherited this greasy spoon." She chuckled at her own description of the café. Her laughter was like the tinkling of fine crystal.

I was enamored. What else can I say?

"You have my sympathies. Vinnie was a great guy. He was always friendly and energetic. We talked a lot when I came in," I said.

It was after the breakfast rush and still too early for the lunch crowd. The place was deserted. Vinnie's old radio in its red Bakelite case sat on a shelf he'd built above the cash register. It softly played swing music. Vera hadn't changed the station on the radio either.

I felt at home and comfortable, even on that lumpy stool.

A tinkle of the bells on the door behind me let me know someone else was coming inside. I glanced up to see two women walk in. They were reflected in the glass surface of the occupancy permit hanging on the back wall. Strolling in, they claimed one of the side tables.

The smell of Pine-Sol intensified. I felt the hairs on the back of my neck stand on end. Aidan was here somewhere. I knew the mystery was about to deepen.

Vera took two glasses, filled them with ice cubes, and poured chilled tea from a pitcher that she pulled out of the fridge. She carried the glasses over to the women.

They must be regulars.

She left the menu on the counter beside my elbow when she

walked away. I'm sure she was hoping I would browse through it while she was gone and see something else that I wanted to order; something more than just the coffee.

She has a good business head on her shoulders.

While she waited for the women's orders, I couldn't help but enjoy the view of her shapely body as it reappeared from beneath the bulky apron.

An intense and overwhelming smell of antiseptic and bleach almost obliterated the aroma of my coffee.

"*She's so beautiful,*" Aidan LeClerc whispered in my ear as he interrupted my train of thought.

Uncle Aidan was definitely here and was spot-on correct about Vera.

As an uncle, Aidan was an intimate part of my past. I had to consider him as part of my present intuitive inner self to be able to handle him being so near to me. He was so cloyingly annoying otherwise, but I was stuck with him. I think he attached himself to me because he thought I wasn't neat enough. As a reporter, he had to keep his notes in order and expected the same of me.

I could tell by their resemblance that one customer was the mother and the other was the daughter. As Vera took their orders, the older woman pointed in my general area. Vera turned her head and gave a quick glance in my direction.

Vera walked behind the counter to the workspace and deftly made the women's salads, topping each with half a hard-cooked egg and a couple strips of ham and cheese. She placed the salads on a dark brown tray that already held cruets of vinegar and oil. With practiced ease, she delivered the order. A quick cleaning swipe and she returned the tray to a place beneath the counter.

"*Did you see that? She didn't clean that tray. She hardly touched it. You're not going to eat in here are you?*" The odor of Pine-Sol intensified. Uncle Aidan was irrational about dirt and germs.

I chose to ignore him. Nobody could be as clean as he was. He was so unbelievably annoying.

After Vera replaced the tray and straightened upright, our eyes met. Those lovely green eyes sparkled. Yearningly, I groaned. *If I were only ten years younger....*

As she strode purposefully toward me, she grabbed the pot of coffee from the hot plate and asked, "More coffee, Mr. Two Shoes?"

"Yes, please and just call me Tommy."

She blushed slightly as she poured. I was hoping that she was thinking some of the same thoughts that I was thinking, but when she spoke, I understood it was just because she was confused and not quite sure how to approach me.

"Here it comes," Aidan said.

Be quiet, Uncle. Not now. I was enjoying her nearness.

"The lady over there said you're a policeman and this area used to be your beat."

"I'm retired now, but yeah, I was a policeman."

"Retired... Great." Again, she hesitated. After a few seconds she continued, "My parents have a trailer park in Florida." Another pause, it was as though she was measuring each word that she was going to say. "I know I just met you, but my parents are in a real bind and... well... you said you knew my granddad."

Right then, I had a sinking feeling. I wasn't sure what was coming my way, but I was no coward. I didn't turn and run out of the cafe. I couldn't. I was completely transfixed by those beautiful green eyes and near perfect smile. But suddenly, the stool where I was sitting had just become a whole lot more uncomfortable.

She sat the coffee pot down, then leaned forward, her elbows on the counter. "How would you like an all-expense paid vacation to Florida?" and there was that smile again. I smelled the heady aroma of her perfume and had an inviting peek at her cleavage.

I've done a lot more for a lot less than a beautiful pair... of... great... ah... eyes and a smile.

A cloud of antiseptics suddenly overpowered the aroma of Vera's perfume, then I heard, *"You're hooked. You'd give her anything."* Uncle LeClerc chuckled. There was a note of enjoyment in his voice seeing my discomfort.

"It doesn't matter what she asks, we are going on vacation," Aidan continued. *"Check your baggage,"* Uncle LeClerc paused. *"We're not going to Disneyland are we? I hope not, I get sick on some of the amusement rides. They don't clean them after each rider. Some people actually throw up in them, don't they? I wonder if they clean them after someone gets sick."*

Vera walked away from me to wait on her two other customers and I was left with Aidan. Sometimes life just wasn't fair.

Vera was a savvy person. When she came back she didn't hover over me, but was courteous enough to give time and space to refuse. But how could I refuse her when she kept flashing that dazzling smile at me?

After a few minutes, she came back and finished her story. "My parents' tenants are threatening to move out. They're having problems with vandals and petty pilfering. The thefts seem too small for the police to take too seriously and the vandalism is mostly the dumping of trash cans in the yards."

I nodded. I understood fully. Some crimes had to take precedence over others because of the severity of their nature. The limited manpower had to be directed toward solving the most serious infractions of the law. It wasn't that they weren't important, they were just less pressing.

"I talked with Dad this morning. He has a nicely furnished, vacant, doublewide unit. He's still looking for someone come down and find out what is going on. He needs to have the thefts and damages to stop."

"Just pack it in," Aidan interrupted. I knew he was enjoying this. He loved to see me squirm. *"We're going to Florida and don't forget to buy more Lysol spray."*

Aidan was already shooting me clues. I wanted to turn it down so badly. I really wanted to say no just to piss Uncle LeClerc off, but... the dazzling smile below those long-lashed, emerald eyes changed my desire to say no and gave her the answer of yes.

"I think I can help," I finally replied. I wasn't particularly happy at all with myself right then; however, I was still a detective.

Her dazzling smile went to blinding in an instant. "Oh, thank you so much!"

She tore a sheet of paper from her order pad and scribbled a telephone number on it. Above it she had written the names of Ina and Darrel Polanski. I knew by the area code, it was near Lakeland and Lakeland wasn't known for being a crime center. It was usually a quiet, crime free residential area southwest of Orlando.

※

Vera's parents picked me up at the airport in Orlando. Ina and Darrel led me to their 1993 powder blue Cadillac Deville. I tossed my filled duffle bag into the expansive trunk. Its size was what was called a two body trunk. As Darrel unlocked the car, I noticed Vera had her mom's eyes and her father's flaming red hair.

I climbed into the back seat. The air conditioning was soon cranked to just shy of frigid. Ina turned to me from the front and chatted the whole way to Lakeland.

"Our older guests come here to relax after they've retired. They can't handle the stress of this crime spree. They're threatening to leave. We've had someone dumping trash over the yards and small things being taken. Nothing big, you know, but that causes them to worry."

It made me smile. *Vandalism and petty thievery as a crime spree?*

Darrel drove five miles under the speed limit. He explained, "Damned old women drivers down here, I almost wrecked this baby," he patted the steering wheel of the vintage car and shook a fist at the thought of his Caddy being damaged, "when one of them pulled out in front of me. I was doing sixty-five."

"Now, Darrel," Ina cooed. She reached over and placed a calming hand on his forearm.

I was watching out the window and almost missed hearing Ina say to Darrel, "When I got the mail this morning, there was a charge on our credit card. You didn't buy flowers for anyone, did you?"

When Darrel said, "No," Ina murmured, "That's strange." There was a slightest hint of jealousy and disbelief in her voice.

"*I think we need to move down here,*" Uncle LeClerc interrupted. "*I haven't seen a tunnel and nothing is very high down here, unlike Pittsburgh.*"

Aidan's arrival surprised me. He hated to fly. Since I had to fly to Florida, I thought that he would have stayed behind.

※

A Soft Spot for Redheads

We drove up to the gates of their property. To one side was a plaque announcing that this was the Darlington Estates. Ina explained, "We bought this land from Mr. Darlington and we thought that his name sounded classier than Polanski Estates." She chuckled at her own joke about the chosen name. Her laugh tinkled, but it was only faintly reminiscent of Vera's.

My accommodations were very nice. *If all their rental units are like this, they shouldn't be losing renters.* Thankfully, Darrel had turned on the air conditioner in the unit before picking me up. It was a relief from the humidity and heat that lurked outside. Fully furnished, it contained a large kitchen, living room with a flat-screen television, dining area, small office area or bedroom, and a master bedroom. I tossed my bag onto the queen-sized bed, turned on the television and began to unpack. I wanted to get settled before I began my investigation.

Aidan appeared in a cloud of antiseptic. *"Don't unpack until you've used the Lysol spray. I saw a 7-Eleven on the way in. You have the money or use your debit card. I want you to buy some cleaning supplies and clean in here, especially before I go into that bathroom or sleep in that bed."*

That's my bed, I countered. *I don't know where you're going to sleep. You weren't invited to come with me anyway.*

Aidan disappeared, leaving the pungent odor of Clorox behind. *Another clue I'm sure, Aidan, but I wish you were more helpful with your clues.* I was starting to know my Uncle Aidan LeClerc better and just knew he was smiling at my comment.

It was evening when I finally emerged from my den. Cooler, I made my first walk around the trailer park. I needed to know the lay-out of the community. It wasn't like any other trailer parks that I'd ever seen before. Each unit was neat and landscaped with a Macadam driveway, outdoor lighting, a car port, and a small storage shed. Vera's parents have made a nice place for people to retire. *Don't get any ideas, Uncle Aidan. I'm not a snowbird.*

Inside of a fenced area was a small, in-ground pool. Many of the guests were relaxing, chatting, and a few were actually in the pool. The parking area around the outside of the pool was filled with golf carts. *A gathering at the water hole,* I thought.

I stopped and introduced myself, telling the story that I was thinking of retiring here. Several of the pool guests spoke to me and I began to learn the residents' names.

I noticed one man, younger than most, circulating among the ladies. He appeared dapper and seemed to think he was a lady's man. I found out later that his name was Ted Kellinger. With all of the ladies eyeing and inspecting me, I felt like a new rooster in a hen house. Apparently, the rumor that I was single preceded me.

Many of the women were widowed and seemed to show an intense interest in me as a newcomer. After quick introductions, I excused myself, saying I didn't have a bathing suit and couldn't join them. Mimi, a lady who was wearing a bright pink bathing suit, said, "You could just swim au natural. We won't look, will we ladies?" I left the pool area amid girlish peals of laughter. I knew that I was blushing and that Aidan was snickering at my embarrassment.

Every morning began with a leisurely stroll through the park and another one every evening. It set a routine for me and it allowed me to observe the activities of other residents in the park. Most of the time, as the sun became less intense and the air started to cool, the residents gathered around the pool. Ted and Mimi, the gal in the pink bathing suit, were there most of the time. I wanted them and the other residents to know I had a regular schedule, but sometimes I walked through Darlington Estates at odd hours of the night when the residents wouldn't see me. Nighttime was when most of the crimes happened. After a week, I was still no further ahead in solving the case.

Whenever Mimi saw me walking by the pool, she'd wave and call, "Come on in, honey, there's plenty of room for you. You don't need to wear swim trunks." And then she'd cackle.

※

There were fifty units in the gated community. The gates told me exactly what Ina had shared with me; the renters were older and needed to have that feeling of security. It was up to me to see that that feeling of safety wasn't being eroded.

I nodded at a lavender-haired woman who whizzed past me in a red and white canopied, electric golf cart. The peacock colored scarf around her neck fluttered behind her. She returned the greeting with a wave of her hand.

"Being neighborly?" I was surprised. It was Dr. Walters who spoke to me. The doc had been Aidan's therapist. It was the first time that he had ever appeared and I didn't know what to make of it.

I heard Uncle Aidan say, *"I don't mean to be rude with you, Doctor, but don't interfere with our investigation. You can stop prying into our business right now. I am giving the clues and I am the one who will be sharing any statements with Tommy. I am his partner."* What surprised me the most about Aidan's appearance was that he presented himself without his germicidal smell.

I ignored them both, but kept what Aidan said in mind, his clues eventually do help, but only after he has tossed so many at me. I wished I could understand him better, find that common thread much sooner, and know what a clue is and what is not.

Neither my uncle nor Dr. Walters responded to help me decide what was a clue.

※

Most people at Darlington Estates owned and used golf carts, but there were a few who still walked. The people who walked, were usually with their dogs on a leash in one hand and a pooper scooper in the other as they made their frequent forays through the park.

There was one exception to that rule. It was a wizened lady who wore huge sunglasses, a golf visor, shirt, and baggy slacks. She was always dragging one of those foldable, wire grocery carts behind her. She would wave and smile every time she saw me.

"Much too friendly, don't you think? She seems to be everywhere we look. She is a bit odd, maybe a bag lady." Again, it was Dr. Walters who spoke.

"Doctor, it's not just her, he needs to check everyone out," Uncle LeClerc insisted. He was trying to take back this case and his position as my partner.

※

I found Darrel outside of the small community pool. He was doing the daily cleaning and maintenance.

"It looks like he's skimming the pool. Finally, someone who is cleaning up things around here," my uncle sighed. *"Watch him and be sure he cleans it really well or you are not going into the pool."* The chlorine smell of the pool only intensified with Aidan's bleach fumes.

More clues, I was sure.

A Soft Spot for Redheads

I asked Darrel about the lady with the cart. He said that she was a resident and her name was Hilda. "She's a bit odd, but she's quiet and walks around the park at all times, even at night."

Darrel put down the pool skimmer and continued by saying, "Last night, a carriage lamp at the end of a driveway was damaged and had its light bulb stolen. The trash cans were overturned and the garbage was tossed through the yard."

Aidan mouthed, *"I certainly hope you don't expect me to go through trash with you looking for clues. If you do, you're out of your mind."* Lysol fumes edged in.

It was then Dr. Walters stepped in, *"Aidan, now you are treading on my area of expertise. One who has mental problems is not necessarily out of his or her mind."*

"It's always been petty things like that. I can't call the police for such small crimes," Darrel continued. "In the past month, we have had a bird bath tipped and cracked; a pair of plastic flamingos disappeared,…"

Dr. Walters cheered, *"Good riddance. Anyone who wants pink flamingos in their yard is eccentric and borderline psychotic."*

"…another couple had a patio chair come up missing, and all of them had their trash cans dumped out." The bright sun made me squint my eyes as we talked.

"There is no safety here. They rely too much on the fence and the gate," Uncle LeClerc reminded me. *"Even at the pool and at social gatherings, there's absolutely no security here at all."* Changing the subject, Aidan said, *"I'm feeling hot. Check my forehead. Do I feel hot to you? I'm not well."*

※

I was starting to learn more names. The couple in the rental unit to the right of me was Carolyn and Monty. The couple to my left was Chuck and Sally. There were no homes directly across the street. It was just a narrow strip of grass and the usual hurricane fence of twisted wire. When I glanced out my window, I saw the grocery cart lady, Hilda, walking along the street.

"She always has that shopping cart." The good doctor popped in and was gone again before Aidan could complain.

Maybe she's been shopping. There's a 7-Eleven just down the street. I bought T.V. dinners and a tin of coffee there earlier.

Darrel cornered me the next day. "A pair of boots was taken from a porch and some rose bushes were trampled last night."

It was time to buy some three by five cards and begin a storyboard, but I needed more information.

"I want to sit down with you and Ina, Darrel." My recent patrols and observations gave no insight into the criminal. "Can I talk with both of you?"

"Climb in," Darrel said, patting a spot beside him in the golf cart. With a bump and a buzz, I found that we were pulling up in front of his office a few seconds later.

Darrel called, "Ina. Can you come here?"

"Coming, honey."

"Make sure you're decent. We have company."

I heard a familiar laugh echo down the short hallway.

When she arrived, "Oh, it's you, Tommy. Any news?"

"I haven't seen anything out of the ordinary and since this is a gated community," I said, "it has to be someone who has access to the place and is free to come and go. If it's not someone coming in, then it would have to be someone you wouldn't expect, an inside job. We have to look at everybody. Unless we can catch a person in the act, this case is not going to be easy to solve. The

A Soft Spot for Redheads

vandalism and petty pilfering may only be a tip of an iceberg. Because these crimes are so persistent, there may be other things going on behind the scenes. We need to check on everyone."

"What can we do to help?" Ina asked.

"I need the two of you to look through your books for me. I hope that you've kept notes on the dates and locations of the crimes?"

"No, not really," Darrel said.

"Then, I want the two of you to sit down and patch together a list for me."

I made another circuit around the park before heading back to the air conditioned comfort of my digs.

Just before I reached the mobile home where I was staying, Dr. Walters made another appearance. *"There's Hilda. She's certainly not a neat person or very pretty. I wonder what she has in her cart, Tommy."*

"I'll give you that she's not neat, Doctor. Great intuition, not really," Uncle Aidan said sarcastically. *"Now let my nephew alone or you'll pull back stubs,"* Aidan warned. For some reason, he was more irritated than normal. It certainly wasn't like him nor was it his normal doctor/ patient relationship. But, maybe it was just his way to slip in another clue.

I could hear the doctor giving my uncle a raspberry. *"P-f-f-f-f-f-t!"*

Doctor, that isn't very professional of you.

"We were having a session," Dr. Walters explained, *"when you pulled us both away. Try dealing with that man, twenty-four hours a day and see how professional you are. You only have him occasionally popping in and out of your life."*

I couldn't argue with that and changed my direction to intercept Hilda. What could a look hurt?

I stopped her just to "chat." I sidled closer to her. She had a gravelly, leathery voice and was five-two about ninety-five pounds, stringy, mouse colored hair. She was wearing the same clothing that she wore the first day we met. The sunglasses and visor hid her eyes. I shifted my position and glanced inside. The cart had a folded up newspaper, a few aluminum soda cans, and some empty plastic bags from the 7-Eleven store.

If she's a thief, she's certainly not getting much.

"Have you ever watched T. V.? She's a **hoarder**." I was surprised. My thoughts and Aidan's voice melded on that last word, but I had never heard him be so blunt before, if it was a clue.

Darrel dropped by my unit later in the day and said, "I had some more reports come in today. There were more trash cans tipped over and the garbage spread over their drive."

In a whiff of antiseptic, my uncle pleaded, *"Anything but trash, Tommy. Please, no trash. I can't do garbage."*

"It has to be Hilda. All of the clues are pointing at her. Even the contents of her cart incriminate her," Dr. Walters said.

I shared my suspicions with Darrel. "I can't do surveillance on her. There's no place for me to hide near her home. She comes out of her house at all hours. I'd be spotted in a second. If I tailed her, someone would report me as a stalker. Is there any way we could gain entrance to her unit without arousing her suspicions?"

"Well," he drawled. "It's not quite time, but I can get Billie the exterminator in to spray beneath each house. I have him check inside the homes for infestations twice a year. Once in the spring and once in the fall, I'll have to check with his schedule and then give the residents a few days' notice."

"You know Billie the exterminator?" I said. I'd occasionally seen the program on the television.

A Soft Spot for Redheads

When he nodded yes, I asked, "Isn't that expensive?"

Darrel laughed. "Not really. It's been a set price for years. If he finds anything to film, I get free advertisement on his T. V. program and he has a paying job. It's a win-win situation for both of us. We were on his program last year when a huge water moccasin decided to move into the pool."

I chuckled and said, "Good deal."

"*Bugs! Snakes! Infestations! Let's go home. I don't think I can handle this anymore.*" A sudden burst of Pine-Sol matched his eruption of emotion.

After his initial tirade, Uncle LeClerc settled down and was quick to remind me, "*Make sure he checks the bills and the invoices from Billie. We can't trust anyone here.*" The smell of household cleanser mellowed.

Those clues puzzled me and made me feel more certain that I was on the wrong track with Hilda, but we had already set those wheels in motion. I was missing something. Not everything was jiving. The information that Adrian was giving was not falling into place with what I was seeing nor with the clues that Dr. Walters was giving me.

Billie came. Hilda's place was inspected. She was definitely a hoarder. We only found trash. Aluminum cans, plastic bags, stacks of newspapers, and magazines were piled everywhere in the unit. Among the stacks and piles, we found the pair of pink flamingoes, the porch chair, and the pair of boots. Darrel warned her that he would evict her if she didn't allow him to get rid of all of the accumulated trash and suggested that she should seek psychiatric help.

"Psychiatrist? Did I hear someone mention psychiatrist? That will be $200.00 for the initial consultation, please." The doctor was in.

All of the trash was removed from the rental unit. Hilda said that anything she had collected was left by the garbage cans. Anything that she thought was being tossed out, she kept.

The pair of boots, the lounge chair, and the flamingos were confiscated and returned to their owners. Her unit was a bit worse for the wear, but with trash removal, a complete cleaning and repainting, it would be ready for Hilda's return.

※

Now, I was no closer to solving the case than when I first arrived. I rethought my clues and recalled what Hilda had said, "I don't dump the things out of the cans. I just pick up the aluminum cans, magazines, and newspapers out of the garbage when the trash bins are already spilled over or I pick up the things that are tossed to the curb. I found the chair and the boots in with the spilled trash. The flamingos I liked and claimed them for my own."

I walked to the 7-Eleven and bought another package of three by five index cards and several ballpoint pens. It was time to re-examine Aidan's clues. Dr. Walters' interference had helped guide me down the wrong path. I could hear Aidan giving the doctor the raspberries this time.

Back in my rental unit, I recopied Aidan's clues onto the index cards and spread them on my table. I even looked the clues from the doctor I'd made earlier. I made two stacks. I checked the doctor's clues first. They all pointed to Hilda. I laid those aside.

I began to spread out Aidan's clues and started to see a thread throughout them dealing with finances. There was a hole. I needed the information that I asked the Polanski's to gather for me. Hoisting myself up from my seat, I walked to the office to

A Soft Spot for Redheads

see if the Darrel and Ina were home. They were in and Darrel greeted me.

I brought along a map I had drawn noting each of the housing units in the park and who lived in them. I also drew a page of grids to list dates and places where the reported crimes had occurred. We went over the gathered names, any recent changes in life style, or financial difficulties that would have started before the vandalism began. When we were through, I had a better picture of everything that had happened. Dates covered the addresses on my map and the items stolen filled my chart. I said, "I think I have all that I need for now, but I can't tell you until I am absolutely sure."

Back in my mobile home, I tossed the good doctor's cards in the trash.

"It's about time you did that, Tommy. Dr. Walter doesn't understand the first thing about what clues are. I think he just wanted to collect his counseling fee for visiting Hilda. Tossing them in the trash is the right place for those poor clues."

I copied the dates and crimes on my index cards. I was able to pinpoint one home near the center of the crimes and the dates and occasions spiraled out from it.

A much mellowed odor of Pine-Sol drifted in. Adrian was back and was spot on with his new clues. Now I had to figure out how to catch the thief in the act.

I made my rounds, paying special attention to one unit near the center of the park. It was necessary for me to find a place where I could observe that house without being seen.

Bingo, there it was. It was a great spot. I headed home to gather the things that I would need for my stakeout.

※

I noticed from the dates and locations of the crimes and garbage dumps that they had started near Ted Kellinger's trailer. Slowly, the crime scenes and dates radiated outward from there. The victims of the vandalism were only ever targeted once, then the vandal went on to other homes in the community. That had to be the key to the answer. But I needed evidence.

Ted was prime rib for the single ladies. He was a widower and young, too. Six-two, one forty, with slicked back silver hair, a pencil thin moustache, and eyes so dark they looked black. I already knew that he fancied himself a ladies' man, but Darrel said that it was more pronounced after the death of his wife. He reminded me of an old-time, snake-oil salesman.

His name also came up when I talked with Darrel to see if anyone had a change in his or her financial status. Things were tight for him after the death of his wife, but had recently turned around. Medical bills had almost bankrupted him.

The one end of the swimming pool had a good view of Ted's place. I borrowed the key for the pool from Ina, packed some coffee and a sandwich and waited until night had fallen to slip inside of the fence after I'd unlocked the gate. The entrance to the pool closed at ten p.m. There would be no swimmers. Pulling one of the pool's deck chairs over into a shadowed area, I sat where I could watch Ted's trailer without being seen. I began my stakeout.

It was a little after midnight. I heard a furtive sound and saw the porch light turn off at Ted's home. A soft squeak of a door opening and then a latch clicking, he shut the door quietly behind him. Those were the only sounds other than the cicadas. I saw him look around, up the street and then down. Dressed in dark clothing, he was almost impossible to see. The sneakers on his feet only made a noise when he stepped on a stray piece of gravel.

A Soft Spot for Redheads

I slipped out of the unlatched gate of the pool and followed him. By staying just out of sight and on the thick grassy lawns, I was almost as silent as he was.

He started down my street. He couldn't be that stupid. Everyone knew by then why I was there. But being a successful thief doesn't mean you have smarts. He stopped and peered around before dumping Chuck and Sally's garbage. Using a small flashlight, he sorted through the papers and pocketed a few pieces. Leaving the scattered mess behind, he moved on to my cans.

There was nothing in there but empty T.V. dinner trays, coffee grounds, and empty plastic soda bottles.

Ted shook the trash from my cans, but quickly abandoned them for better picking at the next house. I needed more evidence than just the papers from only one trash bin.

He dumped the next can. Just after he collected a few papers from Carolyn and Monty, I yelled, "Hold it right there, buster," and, of course like any other thief, he ran. He was aimed away from his house and that's the way he ran. I was sure that his home would be his destination. I turned around and headed back the path I'd just traveled.

Squatting down in the dark beside the pool fence, I nabbed him as he ran by. Twisting his arm up behind his back, I marched him to Darrel and Ina's place. I couldn't let go of him, so I kicked at their door. Lights snapped on and Darrel yelled, "Who's there?"

"It's Tommy. Open up. I have a present for you."

Once inside, I duct taped Ted's hands together. I knew that Darrel would have tape. All supers and managers had duct tape on hand. Darrel called the police. I showed Darrel and Ina what Ted had been collecting from the trash cans. There were check stubs, paid bills, receipts, and even a bank statement with social security and other personal information listed.

"I think Ted's been making his money by using the identities of your tenants and gathering the information to make purchases and siphon off cash from their banks. You may want have the residents double check their bank statements and credit card bills. While you're at it, Darrel, you may want to check your own statements. I heard Ina say while we were driving here that she was concerned about a purchase on your credit card."

The police arrived, got a search warrant, and found the discarded and stolen information that Ted had been using to bilk money for his man-about-town lifestyle. They also found newly issued credit cards and applications for several more. He had been skimming a little here and there, so the thefts would less likely be noticed. When Billie the exterminator came, Ted had enough of a warning to secret away all of the illegal documents and credit cards before the inspections and fumigation.

The case was solved, but I still had a week until the end of the month in my rental unit.

Enterprise picked me up in bright red Chevy Malibu. I spent my remaining time on the beach.

I was glad I had discarded Dr. Walter's misleading clues. *Thanks for your help, Doc,* I said sarcastically.

I settled back to relax in the sun on a soft beach chair with a tall glass of iced coffee.

Uncle Aidan whined. His Pine-Sol almost ruined the fresh smell of the ocean breeze and my coffee. *"What about me? I kept giving you the right clues. If you'd have listened to me a lot earlier, we could have been home by now. You know I hate getting sand in my shoes and do you know what fish do in that water?"*

You're getting better, too, Uncle, but this is my vacation. Now, grab a lounge chair and be quiet.

A Soft Spot for Redheads

"Oh, there's girl in a yellow bikini. I can't look." Aidan covered his eyes and turned his head away. He was uncomfortable with seeing bare flesh.

Me, on the other hand, I was enjoying the view.

Crime Hits Home

I wanted to write mysteries, but every time I've tried, I got caught up in a real life mystery. Even Vera involved me in a mystery.

Vera hadn't changed the name or much of anything else inside or outside of P's Cafe after her grandfather, Vinnie Polanski, died. She worked there helping him as he grew older and the cafe was her inheritance. After my first meeting with Vera, a shapely, buxom redhead, I was entranced. Her smile enticed me into solving a crime wave of petty vandalism for her parents. However, the crime turned out to be much more.

Since then, I'd made it a habit to drop into the cafe near closing time for a cup of coffee and to keep an eye on her. Vera was not hard on the eyes at all. She stood about five eight, weighed in at one-hundred twenty-five, and had the most gorgeous smile and emerald green eyes that I had ever seen. Her tight jeans only accentuated her slim waist and feminine bottom. It was better than sitting alone, watching T.V. in my apartment.

A coincidental meeting with her, as I became reoriented with my neighborhood, soon became a good friendship.

Late every evening, I stopped in to visit her in the cafe. It became my routine. I would claim one of the red Naugahyde topped stools at the counter and relax for about an hour or so before I headed home for the night. I sat on my perch and talked with Vera as she got ready to shut down.

Once, I offered to walk her home after she closed up shop, but she just laughed. "I live upstairs, Tommy. There's no need for that." Oh, how I loved that laugh. It tinkled brightly like crystal prisms of a chandelier stirred by a soft breeze.

"You mean I can't play hero with you, then?" I quipped, disappointed.

She laughed again, "No, but maybe some other time you can help me. Thank you for the offer though." She put her pale, dishwater wet hand on mine. I felt my mouth go dry. It was the first time she had touched me other than our introduction handshake. "I do appreciate all you've done for me and my parents."

It was like that between us. Not boyfriend. Not girlfriend, but becoming fast friends. I enjoyed the view, the conversation, and the company. She tolerated me and sometimes, I guess that was all an old man could ask.

※

It was almost closing time and Vera was cleaning the grill of the cafe. My butt cheeks hung over the sides of my usual stool like saddlebags on a bike. Those stools were not the most comfortable things to sit on, but I endured the discomfort willingly. The reward for sitting in that exact spot was that I had an unobstructed view of Vera as she worked behind the counter.

Soft music played on the small, red Bakelite radio that old man Polanski had bought. He'd built a shelf for it above the cash register.

What a great way to end the day, I thought, but fate was about to show me how wrong my thinking would be.

The tinkle of the bells on the door behind me announced the arrival of a customer.

It was a bit late for customers. Automatically, I glanced up to see a reflection in the glass framed occupancy permit on the back wall. I barely had a chance to glimpse two figures wearing dark hoodies behind me before I felt a glancing thump on my head. My sight exploded into a myriad of stars and flashing lights.

When I woke, two paramedics hovered over me. I was flat on the floor of the café, looking at the pressed tin ceiling. My best shirt was cut into ribbons and I had a horse collar around my neck.

"What in the…?" I tried to get up.

One of the paramedics put a restraining hand on my shoulder and said, "Don't move, sir. We have you strapped to a backboard. You have a head injury. We found you unconscious on the floor."

I growled, "Hell, yes. You get thumped on the head and see if you don't end up on the ground."

When I saw a small smile on his face, I knew that I wasn't going to die.

I heard a familiar voice just out of my sight say, "Still that crabby old cop, I see."

Even though I was immobilized, I didn't need to look to know that it was an old friend from the police force. "Marty, is your screwy partner here, too?"

"I am and I resent that." Dave laughed.

I returned my focus back to the medical personnel. "I need yinz to get me out of all this rigging and horse collar. I'm not hurt that badly."

"For your safety, we want to take you to the hospital. There's a cut on the back of your head that will need stitches."

Stubborn old coot that I was, I refused the ride in their ambulance. They had me sign a refusal of treatment before I could get them to remove everything—including the I.V., but I did leave the bandage on my head in place. I felt like a bat hanging upside down trying to sign the form while I was strapped down on that board.

When I stood I felt dizzy, so I grabbed the nearest stool and sat down quickly. Noticing some blood on the countertop, a feeling of dread seized my heart. *Vera!*

I turned to Dave and said, "The woman that was here, is she okay?"

"She was shot. It was high on her shoulder. She was already taken to the hospital."

"Do you know how she is?"

"It's too soon for me to know. She left about ten minutes before you came to," Marty said.

Blood started to trickle from under the bandage on the back of my head and down my neck. I reached back to put some pressure on it. *Ouch, that hurts.* Maybe I would go to the hospital, but later, on my own terms.

Aidan LeClerc, my uncle and my ghost partner, appeared in a cloud of Lysol disinfectant spray. *"What did you expect, Tommy? Because you liked the view on your stool, you allowed someone to get behind you and tap you on your head. You're a cop. How could you allow yourself to end up on that dirty floor? She hadn't even swept in here yet."*

Not now, Uncle. I'm not in the mood. I'm not feeling up to anything right now.

This was the first time I'd ever been a victim and it sucked. It really sucked.

※

Marty and Dave had no more information about Vera. They kept me at the scene long enough to take my statement before allowing me to leave. The delay in finding out what was happening with Vera and the way my head felt almost made me regret that I hadn't taken that ambulance ride. I would have been closer to Vera. Hanging around the café would only contaminate the crime scene more than I already had. But then, I was part of the crime scene.

I hailed a cab. That was no small feat for a guy with a bloody, bandaged head and a tattered shirt. I considered it a small miracle and headed for the hospital to have my head examined. *No comments about me seeing a shrink, Aidan, and having my head examined.*

"You were really out cold," the ghost of my uncle LeClerc commented. He used to be a police reporter and thought he knew everything about crimes.

"I told you, I am not in the mood for clues right now. Tell me tomorrow."

The cabbie glanced back at me and said, "You talkin' t'me, mac?"

I apologized, "I was mumbling to myself." I needed to be careful talking out loud or someone would think I really needed to see a shrink.

On the way to the hospital, I mulled over the incident, reviewing what I had seen. I couldn't give a good description to the investigators at the cafe. I just didn't get a good look at them and everything was still fuzzy. Why was it that I couldn't remember anything more than any other victim of a crime? I was a trained professional. I should have been able to do better.

I arrived at the hospital's E.R. at a good time. The waiting area was virtually empty. A nurse, who saw my bandage, the matted blood in my hair, and the dried blood that had trailed down the back side of my tattered shirt, snagged me, then hauled me off to a treatment area. As the nurse cleaned my wound, I needed to ask about Vera.

While I was being seen in the exam room, I made a plan to give the hospital more information about Vera. I was sure they didn't have I.D. on her and she would have been admitted under "Jane Doe."

I needed to find out how she's doing.

"Did the ambulance bring in a Jane Doe with a gunshot wound to the shoulder?"

Because of H.I.P.P.A legislation, she was hesitant to share any information until I showed her my I.D. as a cop. "I was another victim of the crime and can give you her name and a telephone number where you can reach her next of kin." She didn't need to know that I was retired.

I hadn't called Vera's parents. I knew absolutely nothing about her present health condition. A call from me without information would have caused more concern than it would have alleviated. It would be better for the hospital or the police to update her parents. I could call them later.

When the nurse handed me a pen and piece of paper, I wrote Vera's name and her parents name and telephone number in Florida. It made me feel better, knowing that Vera would no longer be a Jane Doe.

In return, the nurse said, "When the woman came in, she had

a through and through G.S.W. (gunshot wound) in her left shoulder. They took her upstairs and into surgery. She was still in the recovery area the last I knew."

No one was going to see her or talk with her until the morning. I was relieved. At least I knew that she was alive. And that was good enough for me… for tonight. With me wrapped in a hospital gown, a new bandage, and no blood showing, it was a little easier for me to catch a cab from the hospital to my apartment.

※

I awoke late with the worst headache that I ever had.

"*You look really rough, Tommy. Worse than a hangover, I'll bet,*" Aidan LeClerc started. "*Your head has to feel as huge as a watermelon and you look almost as green as one as well. You need to get cleaned up. There's still blood in your hair.*"

Now you're a comedian. Thanks for the sympathy, Uncle. Go lighter on the Pine-Sol. The smell of it along with my headache is making me sick to my stomach.

After I washed down three aspirins with two cups of coffee, I felt half human again. Between the strokes of the razor, I managed to eat some toast with strawberry jam, then I eased into the shower, careful not to get my head wet as I'd been instructed. I combed a lot of the clotted blood out of my hair as gently as possible. Gingerly, I avoided snagging the stitches. I didn't need to create more areas of pain on my scalp. Carefully, I brushed my teeth, not to jar my head.

Heavy clouds filled the sky. Not wanting to get caught in the rain or get my stitches wet waiting for a bus, I coughed up some extra dough to take a taxi. I could hear thunder in the distance.

I gave the cabbie the address for the police station. It was a blessing that this cabdriver wasn't the chatty type. My head just couldn't handle it.

At the station, I wanted to check my statement and look through the information Marty and Dave collected from the crime scene at the cafe. It would make things a lot easier for me to investigate and to possibly jog my memory about some other things that I saw.

Why can't I remember what they looked like? I should be able to recall more. Even if it was only for an instant, I saw their reflection in the glass. I am a professional and should be able to remember more details.

Not only did I feel violated, I felt inadequate, unable to protect myself or Vera. I kicked myself.

Pushing through the glass doors, I entered the lobby of the station, smelling Pine-Sol. Aidan was already here.

Sergeant Duggan sat behind the desk. He called out when he saw me. "Tommy, you old son-of-a-gun, how are you?"

"Not bad for a man who's been run over by a steam roller. You have your nerve calling me old. Have your arteries petrified yet?"

He chuckled an answer, saying, "I heard your hard head has finally come in handy."

It was my turn to laugh, but it made my head hurt. *"It only hurts when I laugh."* How many times had I heard that? I guessed that sometimes it could be true.

"Can I see my statement that I gave for the report last night, Sarge? I was a bit fuzzy then. It may jog my memory." I was sure that he knew that I wanted to see all of the information and because I was an ex-cop, he allowed me to rifle through the whole report.

"If you want to get your clues from someone else and not listen to me,

go ahead, pour over those papers if you think they will help," Uncle LeClerc said sarcastically. The odor of Pine-Sol had diminished greatly and he appeared in a cloud of Lysol.

If I waited for you to give me enough clues to solve the case, the criminals will have died of old age, Aidan.

I settled down at an empty desk to look at the forms in the folder. Other than my statement of two people in dark hooded sweatshirts, there were no other details about the perps. Apparently, the detectives hadn't been able to question Vera yet.

None of the results for fingerprints or blood samples that had been gathered at the scene were back yet or at least hadn't been added to update the file. I returned the folder to Sarge. Thoughts of Vera and the lack of facts in the file made me want to visit her. I didn't think anybody had spoken to her yet and I wanted to check on her. Maybe by questioning her, I could remember more.

"Thanks, Sarge, see you later."

"I'll keep an eye out for you, Tommy."

I walked to the bus stop. A vendor was selling flowers on a nearby corner. I bought a bouquet of mixed blooms. I had no idea which flowers were Vera's favorites. I got to the bus stop just in time to hop on the bus and we were off with a roar and a belch of black smoke.

The sun came out from behind the clouds and the bright sunlight poured through the grime streaked glass of the bus window. *Ow!* I grimaced. The sunshine felt like daggers piercing my brain. I closed my eyes, which was not always a smart thing to do while riding on public transit.

"You brought your sunglasses, I hope," Aidan chided.

It was another clue. Immediately, something stirred in my memory. I forgot all about the pain. I remembered—sunglasses, both of the robbers wore sunglasses. Even though it was dark outside, both were wearing sunglasses. One sported glasses with shiny mirrored lenses and the other wore just regular dark shades. *If I could only remember more of their facial features.* I sat quietly, trying to recall anything else as the bus lurched through the streets to the hospital, but I was fishing in a dry well.

※

At the information desk, I got the room number for Vera. As I walked by the gift shop, I saw a tall glass vase for the flowers. Buying it, I entered the nearest elevator and hit the up button. It wasn't long until I was standing outside her room. I tapped lightly.

"Come in." It was Vera. Her voice sounded rather weak and thin. When I stepped inside, the smile that greeted me wasn't weak at all. The strength of her beautiful smile chased the bass drums that had been painfully pounding, out of my head.

"Oh, Tommy, I'm glad to see you're not hurt."

"I got hit on my noggin, but I'm alive and thankful to see that you are, too. Here, these are for you." I held out the flowers. "I wasn't sure what your favorites were, so I bought a mixed bouquet."

"Daisies are my favorite, Tommy, but these are lovely."

"Let me get some water in the vase." I filled it with water from the bathroom.

Removing the paper wrapper, I placed the bouquet in the vase at her bedside. The room immediately warmed and seemed more cheerful.

A thick, bulky bandage covered much of her right shoulder. Seeing that she was still able to smile, I felt thankful, knowing that she was safe. I also felt a bit guilty at my next thought, but I was relieved all the same. The bullet had gotten nowhere near the feminine attributes that had impressed me so much the first day that we met.

I started with some casual chatter, but the cop in me soon got the better of me and I started to question her.

"I remember that their hoodies were cranberry colored. Both had sunglasses, one was mirrored, the other plain." She recalled exactly the same things that I'd remembered. I nodded in agreement and my head started to replay a bass drum solo. *No more of that.*

"Both of them were about five nine or ten and average weights. I saw light brown hair sticking out of the hoodies of the one with the regular sunglasses, and the other guy had scraggly, black chin whiskers."

"Tommy, the medications are making me a little confused." Vera sniffed. "I can't think of anything more right now, just snatches of what I saw."

I forgot and out of habit, nodded again, understanding. The pounding in my head returned with a vengeance and the headache was interfering with my thought processes as well.

Vera lay quietly for a few seconds and then said, "Mom and Dad called. They should be arriving this evening sometime. They're going to stay until I've mended and can return to work. The doctor said that maybe I could go home tomorrow. They gave me a sling to wear when I am up.

"Granddad told me about a hold-up that he once had at the café. No gun, but the man held a knife. Granddad laughed. The guy robbed him when he first opened up and got practically nothing."

Aidan interrupted, "*I guess this was her initiation, but it was a rough one."* The hospital's smell of antiseptics and cleaning supplies almost masked Uncle Aidan's arrival. Only his annoying, nasal voice announced that he was there.

Ignoring him, I said to Vera, "I'm a cop and I should've had a better eye on them."

"Don't berate yourself. They were behind you and it was only a second or two before the guy with the mirrored sunglasses popped you. Oh!" She said, "Tommy, I just remembered something. They had gold letters on their shirts. I can't figure out what the letters were. I think they might have been a foreign language like Russian or Japanese."

Before I could comment, Aidan put in his two cents worth, *"It's all Greek to me."*

※

Not having anything else to do, I sat in Vera's room as she drifted off to sleep. The thick bandage stuck out from the neck of the cotton hospital gown. I knew she didn't take that bullet for me, but being a cop, even a retired one, I felt that I should have protected her. It was my duty to have watched out for her safety.

I stared at her as she slept, softly snoring. She started to turn in the bed and I saw her wince. That had to hurt. I knew how my head felt. *I wonder if they have any aspirins in this place.*

Restless, I stood and stretched as the sun began to set behind the hills. The last few rays filtered through the dust and grit on the outside of the hospital window. I could see the glow of the lights on the streets and buildings starting to come on, but I didn't much feel like sharing the lighted beauty of Pittsburgh that night. On the river below, I watched the slow progression of a tugboat and several barges moving upstream.

I must have dozed once I sat back down, because the sound of a light tap on the door awakened me. It was Ina and Darrel, Vera's parents. Ina's eyes were red from crying and Darrel looked paler than normal beneath his mop of red hair.

Ina walked over and hugged me. Looking up into my face, she asked almost in a whisper, "Hi, Tommy, how is she doing?" She glanced at the bed where her daughter slept.

"She was shot, but it was high on her shoulder. They say she will be all right. She went into surgery to repair wound last night. The nurses gave her something for pain earlier this evening and she has been asleep since."

Ina squeezed my hand, saying, "Thank you, Tommy, for watching over my little girl."

That hurt. It cut at the roots of my very manhood. I hadn't been able to watch over Vera and protect her last night. Me, the big hero, the one who wanted to walk her home so she would be safe. I couldn't even watch out for myself. Ina's words made me feel even worse than I already felt.

Shit! I felt like such a heel. How did I manage to keep from getting killed as a cop for all those years? I couldn't even protect myself.

A lump rose into my throat that matched the one on the back of my head. I had to get out before I started bawling. Removing one of my business cards left over from my days at the city police from my wallet, I scratched through the number for the police department and scribbled a note. Shaking hands with Darrel, I handed him the card. "My home number is on the back. Call me if you need me." I beat a hasty retreat.

As I rode down in the elevator, it filled with the smell of Pine-Sol and Uncle LeClerc began chanting the song, *"Row, row, row, your boat."*

No more, Uncle Aidan, I have a splitting headache. I can't handle any of your clues right now.

"If you don't like that one, how about, Mary Had a Little Lamb or Four and Twenty Blackbirds Baked in a Pie," he called out in a singsong voice.

I would have rolled my eyes at his antics, but I was sure that movement would have made my headache even worse.

※

When I got back to my apartment, I swallowed three aspirins with a reheated cup of coffee, I settled into my ratty-looking overstuffed chair, then waited for the caffeine and aspirin to kick in. I had almost nodded off when an odor of lemon scented Lysol awakened me.

Yes, Aidan. I can smell that you've updated your arsenal of smells. The lemon scent is much better than the original aroma.

My headache had almost disappeared. *This had better be good, Aidan. I'm tired and feeling really miserable.*

"You could go to see a hypnotist," LeClerc suggested.

See a hypnotist. I would rather see a palm reader or a medium. Are you nuts? I growled.

"Watch it," Aidan said. "Just because I'm a bit neurotic and a ghost, I'm your uncle and that remark is hitting pretty close to my house. A hypnotist can take you back to the exact moment of the crime and have you pull things from your memory. It might just give you a clearer view of the perps and more clues to capture them. If not for yourself, think about Vera."

That did it. The mention of Vera overrode my skepticism. At that point, I had no other viable options, so I decided to chance it. Also, I needed a way to redeem myself from not being able to protect her.

I walked my fingers through the yellow pages: Hubcaps ... Human services ... Humane Society ... Hunting ... Hydraulics ... Hypnotists. Doctor M. Powers PhD and CHt. I circled the number on the page.

※

When I woke the next morning, I felt like I had been run over by a herd of wild horses. My mouth tasted like they'd left a calling card. Although I'd slept in my own bed, my body was sore from sitting in that hard hospital chair and my head was throbbing. The pain was just a little less today.

I called the hypnotist's office. When I explained to the receptionist that I was a police officer working on a case and it was an urgent request, she gave me an emergency appointment for that day. I didn't share with her that I was an ex-cop.

I had no time to waste with an appointment to keep. So I grabbed a shower. The hot water coursing over my muscles helped. I felt almost human again, once I had eaten some breakfast, swallowed three aspirins, and downed a second cup of coffee. I hustled out the door, walking to the bus stop. Aidan didn't need to remind me today to wear my sunglasses. My headache was at a dull throb and I wanted to keep it that way.

I caught the bus, stopping at the police station first to share the conversation I had with Vera the night before with Dave and Marty, giving them all I learned. I then said, "I have an appointment and can't stay." I didn't share that I was going to see a hypnotist, I'm sure they would have laughed me out of the squad room.

I want to get something for my money. I just hope I'm not getting sold a load of crap with a hypnotist, Aidan, I grumbled.

After one bus transfer, I arrived at the hypnotist's office. The building towered mirror-like, built of steel and glass.

A quick elevator ride delivered me to the third floor. I stepped out into a short hallway with an office complex at each end, following the signs to Dr. M. Powers' office. The reception area was as sleek and impersonal as the outside of the place. Stark white walls encapsulated the boxy neutral furniture. Brightly hued patterned abstract paintings lined the walls. They were the only colors in the waiting area. Even the receptionist seemed bland and colorless. It was designed as a place that caused someone not to want to linger. It was "get down to business and leave quickly" décor.

Shortly after I arrived, the receptionist escorted me to the doctor's *"suite,"* as she called it. The doctor was a slender African-American male, about five-six, moderate frame, dark hair, graying at the temples, wearing thick horn rimmed glasses. After shaking my hand, he directed me to sit across from his desk. He picked up my chart that contained the information I had shared with the receptionist. He verified the reason that I was there.

"Let's give it a go, shall we? Would you make yourself comfortable in that reclining chair? Play with the controls until you feel quite settled."

The motorized leather chair had been shaped like a crescent moon. Its leather cover was pale beige and as colorless as the rest of the room. A book lined wall was the only distraction in the entire suite. A few wiggles of my body and a jiggle of the controls and I was set.

"All right, now we can start." Dr. Powers took a seat at my head just out of sight. "Listen to my voice and relax. Take a deep breath and let it out slowly. Again, let it out even more slowly. Relax and rest, close your eyes and breathe slowly. Relax...."

I opened my eyes when the doctor tapped my wrist. "Wake up now. It's time for you to wake up."

It seemed as though I had just closed my eyes. I said, "I don't think it worked, Doc. I still can't remember anything."

"But you did. I record each session and since you'll need it as evidence, I'll give you a copy."

"Did I remember anything?"

"Let me show you." He took a sheet of paper from his desktop and handed it to me. It looked like letters, but they weren't in English.

"You drew these symbols while you were hypnotized. You couldn't describe them, so I had you sketch them. Do they mean anything to you?"

I started to say no, but then it hit me. The clues that Aidan had been tossing my way all along suddenly aligned. *"It is all Greek to me,"* Uncle LeClerc had said. That's what these letters were.

Turning to the doc, I said, "These look like Greek letters like the frat houses and sororities use. Can you tell me which letters they are?"

"Of course, but they're reversed. To see them correctly, you'd have to view them in a mirror. However, I can read them as they are. This letter is Pi. The next is Lambda, and the third is Rho."

Aidan was right again with his inane singing of the nursery rhymes. I just couldn't put the pieces together then. I remembered, Rho Lambda Pi. The doctor had read them as I had written them since I'd seen them in reverse order on the glass of the occupancy permit.

Dr. Powers handed me a flash drive before I left his office.

"Thanks, Doc," I said as I exited his office.

Too antsy to wait for the bus, I grabbed a cab to the police station.

Dave and Marty still happened to be in their office. I showed them my drawing and explained its meaning. The sketch was added to my statement and the flash drive, but I didn't dare tell them what I did to remember the information that was on it.

※

The suspects were quickly identified once the pool of possible perpetrators had been reduced and associated to the one frat house. The fingerprints found at P's Café matched one of the pledges.

He and another young man had been involved in the initiation rites to join the frat house. They were sent out without any money. They were to buy a keg of beer, and return to the house before ten p.m. The underage purchase of an alcoholic beverage was the least of this young man's worries, now.

Marty and Dave questioned him. When he was confronted with the facts and our description of him with his fingerprints at the cafe, he quickly rolled over on his accomplice. His partner had pointed the gun on Vera after he'd hit me over the head. The one with the gun thought Vera was reaching for a weapon or something under the counter. He panicked and pulled the trigger.

The first suspect revealed, "I was so scared when he shot the lady; I pissed my pants. I left the money untouched in the register and took off. I wasn't hanging around for the cops to pick me up.

I didn't do anything."

The D.A. charged both of the young men with robbery and attempted murder. Instead of being inducted into the frat house, they were awaiting trial in a different type of house.

"The big house," LeClerc chimed.

When we heard the good news, Vera, her parents, and I crowded around the counter at P's. We celebrated, opening a bottle of wine I had picked up earlier.

My evening routine had changed. I still came to P's in the evening, but I now sat on a new stool far away from the front door. It was still lumpy, but it was getting more comfortable all the time. The best thing about my new spot: I could still enjoy the view.

The Burden of Love

Dah-da-dum-dum. Dah-da-dum-dum.* The theme from *Dragnet* rang loudly on my cell phone. I swore I'd never own a cell phone, but Vera bought the phone for me. She bought the phone as a thank you gift for solving a problem that her parents were having in Florida and for helping to collar the two men who had shot her while robbing her cafe. How could I refuse a gift from a great and beautiful friend like Vera?

"Tommy, it's Vera."

I felt my bunghole pucker. I knew she had another favor to ask me. I've been trying to write a book about some of my cases as a cop or a fictional mystery, but even before I can get an idea together and down on paper, I'd get tangled in real life mysteries, many centering around her.

"Ed's missing," Vera said.

Vera Polanski was a woman that my dreams were made of. Her long legs and a slim waist were works of art. Five foot eight, one hundred-twenty pounds, coppery red hair, emerald green eyes, and a killer smile. The image of the first time I'd met Vera, flashed through my mind as she popped up from behind the counter of P's Cafe. Her sudden appearance reminded me of Rita Hayworth in the film *Gilda*. I knew that I was too old for her, but it didn't stop me from looking at her menu. Her feminine attributes and great cup of joe were things I imagined an ideal woman to be. She'd definitely made an impression on me. If I were ten years younger or Vera was ten years older, I'd be giving Ed a run for his money.

Ed Richter was Vera's fiancé. I'd met him occasionally. He stood five foot ten, one-eighty, blond hair, and olive green eyes. He seemed to be very affable and highly reliable.

A not-so-subtle smell of Pine-Sol enveloped me. Uncle Aidan had arrived, heralding the beginning of a new mystery. Uncle LeClerc was my muse and spirit of my mother's deceased brother. He chose to partner with me for some reason. Sometimes, I think it was his warped idea of a joke. He was always so precise and clean and he thought I was less than neat. In his own strange way, Aidan fed me clues that helped me solve the mysteries that came my way.

"Ed was supposed to stop by the cafe for coffee before going to work this morning. He didn't show up and hasn't called. I'm really worried," she said.

Vera was the sole owner, sole cook, sole waitress, and chief bottle washer at P's Café. She had inherited the business from her granddad. Its maximum capacity held sixteen diners.

I looked at my watch. It was nearly noon.

"Can you help me, please, Tommy?" I could only imagine the sadness in her sweet, green eyes.

I sighed. I rightly guessed that I was in for another adventure.

"Let me grab a quick shower. I can be there in about twenty minutes," I managed to say.

I'd been struggling with a plot all morning, trying to create

The Burden of Love

the core for a detective story, so I was still wearing my boxers and the t-shirt that I'd slept in. Why get dressed if you're the only one to see what you look like? My ex didn't like me roaming around in my underwear, so right before the divorce, I did it just to tick her off.

"Don't worry about lunch. I'll have it ready with a fresh pot of coffee."

"Fine, see you in a few," I said.

P's Café was only a few streets away along the beat I used to walk during the time I was a street cop. It was a refuge where I'd spent many evenings, since I retired, perched on a lumpy stool, making love to a cup of strong, black coffee.

Pushing open the heavy, glass-faced, wooden door, I was greeted by the jangle from the bundle of bells that hung by a red cord from the door's brass handle.

I grabbed a red Naugahyde topped stool at the green Formica countertop. It was my "new" seat. I'd given up my old seat after I'd been cold-cocked during a robbery at the cafe. My new seat didn't have the same view of Vera as she worked, but it was safer.

Vera finished stacking my burger and dumped the fries hot from the fryer onto a plate. She turned from the grill holding a plate filled with my lunch. The flavor of the food filled my nostrils. She quickly followed it with a hot cup of coffee.

I lifted the cup to my lips and inhaled, enjoying its savory aroma. The odor of Lysol rushed me like a freight train, killing the delicious smells of my meal and my coffee. I could hardly eat my food.

Damn it, Aidan. Why do you always try to ruin every great cup of coffee and meal that I get? I groused.

"Make sure that you get as much information as you can and get a picture of Ed," he said.

Vera's eyes were red from crying. I hated to see any woman cry, but it really hurt me to see her unhappy. I hadn't felt this bad since she had been shot.

Between sniffles, Vera said, "Ed and I talked yesterday afternoon. He said he would stop in early this morning for a cup of coffee and we could talk before he went to work. I picked up some pastries." On a tall stand and under a glass dome of the counter, rested several apple turnovers.

The door opened. A portly man in a gray, pin-striped suit entered. The sunlight glinted off his doorknob head. He took a seat at a side table. "Excuse me," Vera said as she hurried away with a menu in hand. She came back to pour a cup of coffee, then carried it back to the table with a small creamer taken from the fridge. Taking out her pad, she wrote the order.

Washing her hands, she broke some eggs and tossed the cheese and ham on top of the egg mixture. Two pieces of toast popped out of the toaster. Vera folded the eggs over allowing it to fry a little bit more. She plated the omelet and toast, then served it.

Aidan returned in a pool of Pine-Sol. *"I wonder if he'd like a glazed donut, a pastry, or a frosted piece of cake?"*

He was shooting some clues to me, even though there were no donuts or cake in the cafe. I copied his words carefully down on my napkin.

Vera came back to the counter. "Ed works for a window replacement and glass repair company. He's a master glazier. His dad taught him the trade. He worked for his dad while he was in high school. When his dad passed, he went to work for Classiglass. I tried to call him several times this morning and got no answer, and he hasn't returned my calls."

She called to the other customer, "Would you like some more

coffee?" As usual, when a waitress asks if you need anything, your mouth is full. It was the same for the portly man. He could only shake his head, "No."

"I don't know where he is." Vera pulled a card from beneath the counter. "Here is the address of the company where he works." She rightly assumed I would look for Ed. "He is on call twenty-four hours per day, but for emergencies only. That's why he drives the van to and from work." She sniffled, took a napkin, and wiped her nose. She wrote down the address of Ed's home on the back of the card.

I thought of her laugh, soft and melodious, like the soft tinkling of crystals stirred by a breeze. I hated to hear her cry.

She sniffed. "I remember one evening when we were on a date in the van and he got a call. He had to run and replace the mayor's windshield. Ed was on call. According to Classi-glass, it was an emergency. I got to meet the mayor and Ed got a twenty dollar tip."

※

I finished my lunch, limiting my caffeine intake to two cups of java. I couldn't run a risk of having a full bladder while I investigated Ed's apartment building. It was a three story brick structure on a tree lined street in a quiet neighborhood.

I started talking to the neighbors on Ed's floor. I found that no one had seen or heard Ed all last evening or this morning.

Reaching the first floor, the hallway filled with a chlorine bleach odor. Aidan appeared. "Look at this building. It's been remodeled, but they've cleaned and reused all of the original fixtures. The old doors, transoms, and hardware were redone. Look at the leaded glass *doors. They're beautiful,"* Uncle LeClerc admired. *"They used the genuine articles if any had to be replaced."*

More clues, I was sure.

I held the door open for a lady who said she lived in 2-B. She was returning from walking her little mongrel dog. I asked if she had seen Ed, but she couldn't add anything more about Ed's location.

I walked around the block looking for clues or the van. Nothing looked out of place and his van was missing. I strolled through the surrounding neighborhoods checking the alleys, parking lots, and driveways. The Classi-glass van was nowhere to be seen. With nothing to show for my efforts, my next stop was the police station to see if anyone fitting Ed's description had been involved in an accident.

※

"Hey, Sarge."

"Hey, Tommy, I thought you'd moved to Florida. I heard you had a case down there," Sergeant Duggan bantered.

We shook hands. "Not a bad grip for an old man. It must be from hefting that pen all day long."

Sarge laughed, "You aren't out shopping for a walker are you?"

"I'm here on business." I explained the details of my visit, telling him it wasn't a police matter, because Ed hadn't been missing for twenty-four hours, but his fiancé was worried.

"I got nothing for you, Tommy," Sarge said after he scanned the computer screen in front of him, "but if something comes in, I'll give you a call."

"Sarge, could you have the units keep an eye out for the Classi-glass van?"

"Sure will, Tommy."

"You better write it down or you'll forget. At your age, senility is just around the corner," I called over my shoulder.

I walked into a cloud of Lysol as I stepped outside of the station.

Yes, Aidan, I know you're there.

"You'll have a job ahead of you and it won't be as transparent as you'd hope. Some leads may fake you out. Don't be lured away with those false leads. Take care," shared Uncle LeClerc.

More clues, I'm sure. Why can't you be more open?

"I know you think I am a pain, but you can be a pain, too, don't you know. I try to help and what thanks do I get? I am beginning to think that you are jealous of my clue finding ability." The smell of the Lysol disappeared just as quickly as it appeared.

※

I hailed a cab and climbed inside. When I gave the cabbie the address, he called over his shoulder, "Yo, dude, what kind of cologne are you wearing? It smells like bleach and Pine-Sol."

Uncle Aidan had arrived and no one had ever smelled his approach before. Something was up with him. He overheard the directions I'd given the cabbie.

"Tommy, no tunnels. I can't go through a tunnel. Tell the cab driver to go around.

He's afraid. That's what was wrong. *We could go up and over.*

"No, not up and over either. No tunnels and no heights. I will do bridges though," Aidan wailed.

Oh, brother, I had a ghost muse who assigned himself to me

that's afraid of heights and tunnels and I live in Pittsburgh. *Uncle, you have to have a warped and perverted sense of humor to have lived in the city of Pittsburgh with all of your fears. Are you punishing me for something I've done?*

It's southwestern Pennsylvania, Uncle. Get over it. Pittsburgh is nothing but hills and tunnels. How did you ever manage to live here for all of those years? I'm glad that you can cross bridges or I'd have to stay in my apartment with you and order take out. It's too bad you don't like tunnels, but, we're going through. Close your eyes or go to wherever you go when you're not torturing me.

"I'd just leave and let you solve this case on your own, Tommy, but I've grown to like Vera, too. I'll stay for her sake." Aidan and the smell disappeared just before we entered the Fort Pitt tunnel. Classi-glass was located between downtown Pittsburgh and the airport.

When we exited the tunnel, the cab again filled with the odor of Lysol. I saw the cabbie glance back at me in the rearview mirror.

Tone it down, Aidan. I know you're here. What's going on with you today? Everyone else doesn't need to know you're here.

We pulled into the Classi-glass parking lot. I climbed out of the cab and tipped him more heavily than I normally would because he had to put up with Aidan.

"Put up with me? Be careful, Tommy. One more insult or false step and you're on your own. However, if you want the whole picture, you need to gather all of his assignments, follow his steps, see where he went."

Above the door was the sign, "Classi-glass ... Auto glass, stained glass, commercial ... Repairs and replacement." Vera told me that Ed was an expert in replacing, repairing, and creating all kinds of glass. He'd worked with auto glass, leaded glass, and stained glass. He'd done repairs for many of the historical sites and churches throughout Southwestern Pennsylvania.

An older model van with the company logo on the panel was parked to the one side of the building. I was hoping that it was Ed's and that I would find Ed inside with some good reason for missing his morning date with Vera.

The raucous buzzing of an alarm on the door greeted me as I entered the sales room. I hated that sound. It grated on my nerves. Immediately, I felt claustrophobic in the small room, surrounded by multiple displays of replacement windows and a narrow counter that was covered in advertisements, catalogs, and placards.

I was about to chide Aidan for his compulsion to straighten the brochures when my thoughts were interrupted.

"May I help you?" The voice came from a woman who had walked into the showroom from a back area of the building. She was Caucasian, about forty-nine, five foot two, one hundred-thirty pounds with chestnut hair, and hazel eyes—a beautiful woman, more my age.

The door's buzzing and Uncle's fidgeting with the brochures put my nerves on edge, but that view soothed my nerves a bit. She was lovely. Her skin was smooth and her smile was warm and wide. I noticed her ring finger was bare. That gave me some hope that she might just be unattached.

I pulled out my retired police badge, flashed it, and said, "I'm Tommy. I'm here to investigate the whereabouts of your repairman, Ed Richter. His fiancée, Vera, said he hadn't shown up for his usual cup of coffee this morning. She's worried because she can't reach him and asked me to find out if something had happened to him. Was he called out on an emergency?"

"No, he wasn't, and that's not like him. I've been waiting for him to come in for his assignments. I'm Cora, the office manager."

"Is that his van parked outside?"

"No, I have only two technicians, but we keep a spare van. Just in case we have a problem with one of the vehicles, I never want to tell a customer that we can't service them."

"Very nice to meet you, Cora. I am going to need the trip sheets and assignments for Ed covering the past week or a week and a half."

Cora reached under the counter, lifting out a pocketed folder. "I've been worrying why he hadn't shown up for work or at least called me. That's not like him.

"These are Eddie's job orders for this week. I usually enter them in the computer nearer the end of the week. The technicians can figure out costs on site. Some customers choose to pay at the end of the repair. Those who don't, I send out bills that are generated when I enter the assignments in the computer. I'll print out last week's list in a minute. If you need space to go over those work orders, there's a stool there and I'll clear some space on the counter. Be careful not to lose any."

Not another stool. My butt is gonna be shaped like one soon. At least this one has more padding than the ones at P's Café. I pulled out my pad and pen. A subtle scent of Pine-Sol filled the office. I looked to see of Cora was cleaning or, after the cab ride, if she noticed the odor.

Aidan reappeared.

Yes, Uncle.

"Make sure you copy all of the information: names, addresses, phone numbers. No matter how small the detail, finding Ed may hinge on everything that you write down. The facts always helped me when I reported on cases."

The Burden of Love

This isn't my first rodeo, Uncle LeClerc. I'd already planned on doing it.

I chose to use a different page for each client. I would have room for any notes that I decided to make later and simplify the search for information.

"Put them in order, and then start with the newest," Aidan pushed.

I'll get to them all, just give me time. I need to sort them out before I can start to collect the information.

The smell of Pine-Sol strengthened. Uncle LeClerc pressed closer, looking over my shoulder as I wrote. I made sure that I headed each page with a client's name and telephone number. They would be essential for me to start my investigation.

As I left, I said, "Thank you, Cora. Thanks for letting me see your records." I handed back the folder. "I'll try to keep you updated as well. If you hear anything from Ed, please let me know." I handed her one of my cards.

After taking my card, she extended her other hand and shook mine. It felt so soft, but her grip was strong. Her eyes were wonderfully warm and her smile genuine. She took a business card from the counter and wrote something on the back.

"That's my home phone number. If you find out anything, call me, anytime."

I felt a bit tongue-tied, like a school boy meeting a girl for the first time. All I could do was to return her smile. She was closer to my age than Vera and Vera was engaged. All I needed to know now was if Cora had a boyfriend.

※

Back at my apartment, I sat down with my house telephone, a lined legal pad, and a pen at my gray topped Formica kitchen table. The table sat squarely beneath the kitchen window. There were no distractions for me there. My view of Pittsburgh was only a painted brick wall with pigeon streaks. The rent was good even though my view wasn't, so I stayed. I spread the recent lists of Classi-glass customers on the tabletop and started wading through the list, after I poured a cup of coffee.

The last repair that Ed had done before he hadn't been seen or heard from was to replace the lead that secured some of the stained glass in a window at the Knoxville Methodist church. The lead had loosened and was allowing water to leak inside when it rained. I dialed the number.

"Good afternoon, Knoxville Methodist Church. This is Dorothy, how may I help you?"

"This is Tom from the Classi-glass Company. I'm doing a follow up on the service that you received on your stained glass windows. I'd like to ask a few quick questions, if you have the time."

"Go ahead."

"I'd like you to rate our serviceman. Was he courteous and polite?"

"I wasn't here, but the Reverend said he was efficient and cleaned up after himself. I would say that he was good," Dorothy answered.

"Would you use our services again?"

"Most certainly," she replied.

"Were our prices comparable?"

"Yes."

"Thank you for your time, Dorothy. Have a great day."

All of the other calls went much the same way. He was a great technician, prompt and courteous. I knew from the testimonials that Vera was dating a good man: reliable, hardworking, and polite.

Only one conversation stood out. It was Ed's first call of the day and my last call of the repairs that he had made yesterday.

"Hello," said a gravelly male voice.

After introducing myself, I said, "I'm doing a follow-up on the repairs to your garage and kitchen windows. I have a few questions about your service."

With no answer, I continued, "Did you find our service man competent and polite?"

"No," the brusque voice replied.

"I'm sorry, was there a problem?"

"Yeah, he was too nebby."

"You say that he was nosey? Excuse me—" but, I was talking to a dial tone.

Interesting. I scrawled a large star on the page, then folded over the corner of the paper in my notebook to mark it for later reference.

Quickly, I completed calls to the rest of both call lists; I was no farther ahead with solving Ed's disappearance.

As I sat there, contemplating what to do next, a bleach bomb hit my room.

"Let's go," Aidan pressed. *"We need to check out the residence of the man who was so rude on the phone and said that Ed was nosey."*

Those were my exact thoughts, but I needed a reason to visit. I needed a hook, so I wouldn't raise suspicion. Sitting at my table, I tried to devise a way I could approach the address without drawing attention to myself. I wanted to do a walk around the house and neighborhood, too. Then it hit me. I called for a cab.

※

The address of the gravelly voiced grouch was near the Classi-glass company. I remembered there was a sandwich shop in the same small mall area. The cabbie dropped me off at the shop. I went inside and bought a $10.00 gift card before I made the walk to Classi-glass. It was a good time for me to share my progress with Cora, possibly make some progress with her, and explain what I intended to do. I would need her help. It would be nice to see her again. She was certainly a woman who was worth a second look and a second visit.

The irritating buzzer welcomed me to the shop. Cora's smile greeted me. It was as pleasing as the buzzer was irritating. I needed to find out whether Cora was dating or spoken for.

"Hi, Tommy."

"Hello, Cora. I think I may have a lead. I'm going to need your help." I explained my plan and asked to borrow a service man's shirt and cap.

"No problem, Tommy, let me see what I can find."

From the back room, Cora emerged with a shirt and cap. "This is the largest shirt that I have."

"You are getting kind of thick in the waist." LeClerc's voice emerged from a cloud of pine-sol fumes.

I chose to ignore him, but I was glad I had worn dark slacks and dark T-shirt. I would wear the button-down shirt like an unbuttoned jacket.

"I need to borrow one of your clipboards. The place I need to visit is in the neighborhood. I'll walk over to the house and check it out."

Cora handed me a clipboard. As I turned to leave, I heard Cora say, "Tommy." She held out a set of car keys. "This is for the extra van. The customer will need to see it in the street to believe you're working for Classi-glass."

Either she was really worried about Ed or she really trusted me. I felt especially touched. "I'll bring the van and the keys back. And Cora, my feet thank you."

She smiled and said, "Just bring Ed back."

I felt a huge lump in my throat. She trusted me and hardly knew me, but maybe it was just a lot of both.

Taking the keys, I drove through the neighborhood to the address in question. I parked on a curve of the maple lined street where I could see the front and the back of the house. It was a small ranch house painted tan with pale green trim and split a fair sized lot. The lawn needed to be mowed. According to the request for work, there was a detached garage. It had to be on the far side.

Donning the shirt and cap, I parked in front of the house. I could see movement inside of the home through a small opening in the drapes. Picking up the clipboard, I stepped out of the van. After taking a deep breath, I knocked on the door.

Inside, I could hear furtive, shuffling movements, much like I'd heard as a cop when entering a criminals' home. I knocked again.

The deadbolt turned. The door cracked open as far as the safety chain would allow. A bloodshot green eye peered through the opening.

"Yeah?" It was the same gravelly voice that I'd heard on the phone. I could now put the voice with an eyeball.

"I'm from the Classi-glass company and am following up on the poor evaluation of one of our service technicians. I am here to apologize to you and offer you a $10.00 gift card. I need to ask the specific reason the tech had a low rating. We are always looking for ways to improve our service."

"He was nebbing through our house," the eye said as the

door inched shut.

"Excuse me," I interrupted. The door re-opened. "He did have to come inside to fix the back door's window."

"Yeah, but he shouldn't have been snoopin'."

I figured I got as much information as I could get from the eyeball. "I'm sorry. Please accept this gift card with our apologies." I slipped the voucher through the narrow opening.

A darkly stained hand took the proffered gift, then closed the door so quickly, it almost clipped my fingers.

A burst of bleach stench assaulted my nostrils. *"That's ink on his hand,"* Aidan quipped before he and the bleach odor disappeared.

I did a quick drive around the block and neighborhood, paying close attention to the grouchy eyeballs' house. There was a walkway leading to the house and driveway from the alley. Shrubs snuggled close to the rear of the house. I turned the van back to the window showroom.

I parked it back at the side of the parking lot and then went inside to return the keys and to see Cora. Greeted by the annoying buzz, I hurried through the door and closed it so it would stop. I smelled Pine-Sol and Cora wasn't cleaning. I moved to the counter and reclaimed the stool.

Uncle LeClerc, quit that. He was straightening the brochures displayed on the table top. *I don't understand. Why you are acting up? You have never done that before.*

"This place is a mess and just look at the dust on the counter. I wonder when this place last had a good cleaning," he said, as he straightened the pencils, lining them up according to size.

I said quit that. Cora's going to see you.

The Pine-Sol odor faded away.

Thanks, Uncle Aidan.

The Burden of Love

Cora said, "Well, what did you find out?"

I explained what I had seen and told her that I would come back after dark to actually visit the house and see what else I could find. "I need to get a closer look."

"Do you have a driver's license?" Cora asked.

I laughed. "It's a little late to ask me now that I've already driven your van, but yes, I do."

"I was so worried about Eddie. I forgot to ask you. I would do almost anything for that boy. He's a great guy."

"Well, there goes the idea she trusted you," Aidan smirked.

"Vera tells me I'm a great guy, too."

"I'll just bet you are," Cora said. I looked to see if she was being sarcastic.

She didn't seem to be, so I said, "Let me give you another card. I'll write my cell phone number on the back." Taking a pen from the counter, I scribbled it down on the back of my card. "The other card I gave you only has my home number on it. Call me anytime."

I was hoping that she was getting my extra meaning. I handed back the keys to the van. Cora pushed them back at me. "Keep them. You're going to need transportation tonight when you come back to investigate. Just don't moonlight with extra tools in the back."

We both laughed when she said, "Don't be coming back late. My name is Cora Daugherty and if you lose my card, I'm in the phone book."

"I won't need the phone book. I'll keep the card safe," I said, stowing Cora's phone number in my wallet. After sticking the keys in my pocket, I chatted with her for a bit, just some small talk. I thanked her, then drove home to wait the next few hours until dark.

On my way home, I stopped at the café and updated Vera. She had stopped crying and even graced me with a weak smile. "Thanks, Tommy. I know you'll find him."

At my apartment, I gathered all of the things that I thought I would need to do my surveillance. Then I took a nap.

※

Waking up refreshed, I drove to almost the same spot where I'd parked earlier. I wanted to be able to watch the front and rear of the house. Sitting in the darkness, I waited until I knew if there was any activity in the house. I listened as the cooling motor ticked off the seconds. After about five minutes, I left the van, closing the door softly.

The smell of Pine-Sol enveloped me. *"I'm here, Tommy. Go ahead. I have your back."*

Thanks, Aidan, I thought. What could he do? No matter what I thought, I didn't say anything. I didn't want to insult him and have him sulk.

Dressed in dark clothes, a black watch cap, and navy tennis shoes, I acted like an urban ninja. Blending in with the trees and shrubs and avoiding the streetlights, I was almost as silent and dark as the shadows. I walked close to the front of the house, peeping in the front windows. I peered through the crack between the pulled drapes and the slats of a Venetian blind. Two men were moving around inside. They worked at a large machine, but I couldn't figure what it was with such a limited view.

I moved away from the front of the house, so I wouldn't draw attention from the neighbors thinking that I was a prowler. I circled to the detached garage. Peeking through the clean pane of newly replaced glass, I saw the outline of a van. *BINGO.* I may have solved the case of the missing van, but where was Ed?

At the corner of the garage were several trash cans. I lifted the lids. I could learn a lot from things people tossed into their garbage. I called it *Garbology 101*.

Paper scraps filled the first can. I picked up a piece. The texture was smooth and not the feel of the typical copy paper. In the darkness, I couldn't tell why it felt different, but I pocketed it. The second can held paper scraps as well. In the third can, I found used ink cartridges.

They are printing something. I recalled what Aidan had said previously. I rubbed the surface of the paper. A light went on in my head.

They've got to be counterfeiting. I'm sure of it. But, how does this have any bearing on Ed's disappearance?

Creeping to the back door, I cupped my hands around my eyes to get a good look through the window. The fresh putty let me know this was the window Ed had replaced. Light from the room beyond faintly illuminated the layout of the kitchen.

I listened carefully. The sound of a dryer running with loud, clinking sounds filled the room.

They were aging the money. Tossing the newly minted bills into a dryer with plastic poker chips gave the money the appearance of wear and age. It was a standard operating procedure for counterfeiters.

I picked up the faint odor of bleach. "That's not the right way to make money," LeClerc replied.

It's good to have you here with me, Uncle Aidan.

A hallway led off from the kitchen. Stepping down from the stoop, I moved to the next window to investigate. I stood on my toes to get a glimpse of what was inside. Light pouring from a bathroom door left ajar, showed a body on the floor.

Is it Ed? I hope he's alive.

I searched the yard for something to stand on for a better view. Taking the basin off a nearby birdbath, I upturned it behind the shrubs beneath the window.

It is Ed.

I recognized his uniform. He wasn't dead. He was bound with duct tape. They wouldn't have bothered to tie him up if they'd have killed him already.

I needed to call this in. I had the evidence. Ed needed to be rescued and the counterfeiters needed to be apprehended. None of which I could do by myself.

I had just stepped off of the bowl to the ground, when a noise at the back door caused me to scrunch down behind the shrubs. One of the counterfeiters emerged from the back door with a trash bag in his hand. After looking around, he walked to the garbage cans and stuffed the bag inside. He glanced around again for a few seconds before returning to the house. As he reached for the door handle, he stopped on the stoop. His eyes searched the yard.

Did he sense me?

I put my head down so he would only see the top of my head and my black watch cap. I held my breath.

A smell of bleach, Pine-Sol, Lysol, and several other cleaning agents filled the air. My eyes began to water. I lifted my head slightly, wanting to keep an eye on the man. Between me and the guy on the porch, a heavy, misty cloud formed, blurring the man's view.

It has to be you, Aidan. Thanks.

The man suddenly turned and went back inside.

No one answered, but the smell dissipated.

I waited for a few seconds before escaping from the shadows

The Burden of Love

of the shrubs and returning to the van. At that moment, I was certainly glad that Vera had talked me into using a cell phone.

※

"Allegheny County, 9-1-1. What is the location of your emergency?" a voice on the other end of my cell asked.

I gave the voice the address she requested and then asked for a patrol car to come. I briefly explained that I was a retired cop, the situation, and I repeated the address. I exaggerated a bit by saying a man had been kidnapped and could possibly be killed.

"No lights or sirens, please. I'm in a van parked several houses away. Have the patrol car stop and talk with me first. I can explain what is happening."

"I'm dispatching a car right now."

About twelve minutes later, a patrol car pulled up beside the Classi-glass van. Killing their headlights, they got out of the car. They shined their flashlights on me, hands at their unsnapped holsters. I waited until they asked me to step out.

Their lights blinded me. I heard a familiar voice. "Tommy, it's you. If I'd have known, I'd have left my rookie partner at the station."

"Walter, I am so glad to see you." Not literally. My vision was still filled with a bunch of dots from their flashlights.

Walter continued, introducing me to his young partner, Jimmy.

I shook hands and quickly ran through my suspicions. I handed them the ink cartridges and paper scraps.

"How did you find these?" Walter wanted to be sure they weren't gained illegally. He didn't want the evidence tainted and void their arrest.

"It was in the garbage behind the house." Being discarded made the evidence legal.

Walter called for another car. Since he had a rookie, he decided he would need back up to cover both entrances of the house and to safely recover Ed. I didn't know exactly what they would find inside, but I described the layout of the house to them as soon as the other two cops arrived.

"I didn't hear the back door lock when the guy threw out the garbage. It should be easy for someone to slip into the kitchen unheard when there's a distraction at the front door. Standing in the hallway, yinz guys can cover the bedroom and stop anyone from exiting out the back door."

"Sounds like a plan to me," one of the new arrivals said.

"I got the front with Jimmy," Walter said, "He needs more experience before I put him in the path of the probable escape route. When I announce 'Police' at the front door, I know they're going to head out the back. Check the time. We go inside in five."

Staying by the van, I watched as the uniformed patrolmen took their places.

A sudden pounding on the front door shattered the silence. Someone shouted, "Police. Open the door. Police." I heard the front door being kicked in.

From inside the house, I could hear commands being yelled. "Get your hands up. Get down on your knees. On your stomach. Get your hands behind your back." Then, it was quiet. Lights in the neighboring homes began to pop on.

I moved closer to the house.

"Still like the old fire horse responding to the bell?" Uncle Aidan said.

No smell of cleaning supplies. Maybe he burned them all out

The Burden of Love

making the mist for me. *Thanks, Aidan, you really did have my back tonight.*

He didn't say anything. Without the odor, I didn't know if he was still there or not.

The other cops led the suspects to the patrol car and after searching them, the criminals were put inside. Walter and the rookie were leading Ed out of the house. Ed chaffed his wrists and walked with a limping gait. I joined them.

Walter made a call for the detectives and forensics to secure and investigate the crime scene. While we waited for them to arrive, I suggested, "Walter, I can take Ed to the station with me. We both have statements to make and that way you can separate the counterfeiters. There's no use letting them work on an alibi." Once the first detective arrived, we were free to go.

"All right, Tommy. Follow us to the station."

The suspects were kept in separate cars.

I led Ed to the van, telling him his van was parked in the garage. "You won't be able to claim it for a few days until it is released. It's part of the crime scene."

I pulled out onto the street, falling in line behind the parade of police cars.

Ed said, "Thanks, Tommy. Vera has told me so much about how you helped her and her parents. Now I am in your debt, too."

"Don't thank me, thank Vera. When you didn't show for your morning coffee yesterday, she was worried and called me."

"That seals it, I'm going to set a date for her to marry me. And, Tommy—?"

"Yes."

"When she agrees to the date, I want you to be my best man."

"What about me?" Uncle Aidan whined.

I'm sure they'll let you be ring bearer, I conceded.

I handed Ed my cell. He made calls to Vera and to Cora, explaining what had happened to him and that he was safe. I could hear Vera crying on the other end of the phone.

Finished with his calls, he told me, "I repaired the windows in the garage and kitchen. I gave one of them the bill for my work and they paid me in cash, three twenty dollar bills. I just tucked them in the compartment of the clipboard and went on to my next assignment. I had two other jobs to do.

"I sat after my last job to tally my till and to finish the paper work. When I lifted the twenty dollar bills out of the clipboard, they didn't feel quite right. I thought they might be fake. I went back to the house to see if the man knew that the bills were counterfeit and if they would make it right.

"The next thing I knew, they jerked me into the house, put a knife to my throat, and threatened to kill me if I made a sound. They bound me with the tape, covered my mouth, and shoved me down onto the floor.

"I could hear them talking in the other room.

"The voice of the man that had pulled the knife on me said, 'I told you not to break those windows to get inside. I couldda jimmied the doors, but no-o-o, you hadda do it your way. You broke in while I pulled da *For Sale* sign from da front yard. You hadda call a smart repairman and pay him wit'da counterfeit money. We had only two more days of work and wedda been outta here wit'out any trouble.'

"The other voice said, 'So what do we do wit' da nebby repairman?'

"The first voice answered, 'Da Ohio River don't give up its dead so easy. I say we knock him out and drive da van into the river. We make it looks like an accident and we don't get blamed. Once we finish here, we load da dryer and da copier, we leave and we're home free.'

"The other voice said, 'Don't forget to put da *For Sale* sign back in the yard.'

"'You and that damn sign. Well, damn you and that damn nebby repairman, too.'"

※

Vera and Ed exchanged vows in the fall. Their autumnal wedding was beautiful. I had to wear a tux, but I had a ringside seat to the whole affair. Vera was spectacularly beautiful as she walked down the aisle on her father's arm. Seeing her happy, smiling face approach Ed and watching Ed's beaming smile as she approached the altar put a smile on my own face.

Cora was part of the audience, of course. Naturally, she'd been invited, but what made me the happiest? Cora was my date.

Missing

Cora slipped her hand into mine. The warmth of her touch brought me back to the present; a present where I really didn't want to be. The heavy smell of the flowers in the funeral home filled my head with memories that hadn't been stirred in years. The thoughts were of my father, his death, and his funeral. That was where I learned to hate the cloying odor of flowers, especially in a funeral home.

My younger sister, Sarah, and I stood at the side of the casket, greeting visitors. Mom was tucked inside the polished oak box, beneath a pale, pink coverlet. The catafalque was surrounded by a small forest of floral baskets and vases.

In the quiet lull between the visitors, I drifted back to another time—a time of remembering my pregnant mom standing beside my dad's casket. Trembling, she would touch his cold, stiff hand and caress his cheek. My younger brother, John and I were ensconced on a sofa at the side of the viewing parlor. When we became restless, Nana and Pap would take turns guarding us or standing with our mom as she greeted the guests. As a young child, I couldn't understand why Dad was laying in the box and not moving.

That was how I grew to hate the sweet, mingling odor of flowers and I hated being at the funeral home.

Sarah had no memories of our dad. She had been born after our dad's death. John had disappeared as a child and I wished that he could be with us. Mom had always wanted to know what had happened to John. She missed him as much as she missed our father, James.

John had weighed heavily on my mind since my retirement, but Mom's frailness had put any action about finding what had happened to him on hold.

By the time the indoor services were over, grief had blurred the names and faces of the visitors who flooded in to pay their respects. The stress and strain diminished somewhat in the fresh air at the cemetery. After the graveside service ended, Sarah and I said our good-byes. I watched as Sarah laid a rose bud on the lid of the closed casket. I touched the casket lid as I left and whispered, "I love you, Mom. I'll miss you."

※

Once the funeral was behind us, it was time to clean out the belongings from Mom's small apartment. Sarah joined me as we sorted through the few things that she had accumulated. It wouldn't take long. Pots, pans, and most of the furniture were being offered to the Salvation Army. Sarah kept the few pieces of jewelry and Mom's old rocking chair. Sitting in the chair, she rocked and said to me, "Mom used to hold me as she sat in this rocker." She rubbed her hands lovingly over the arms of the wooden chair, shiny with age. Sarah's eyes were misty.

I kept the family Bible, Dad's wedding band, and the quilt that my mom and Nana had made.

"Tommy, you might as well take this box of letters and the papers that Mom saved and thought were important. You're the family historian," Sarah said.

The odor of Pine-Sol floated into the room. Aidan LeClerc, the ghost of our deceased uncle, said, *"That box might be worth sorting through, Tommy. You might find some clues to Johnny's disappearance."*

I must have been Uncle Le Clerc's favorite. When he passed, he connected with me. He didn't make his presence known to anyone else.

Mom's death had prodded me into thinking of searching for John and Uncle Aidan's appearance always heralded the beginning of another mystery that needed to be solved. I had to know what happened to my brother.

"You've always wanted to write. These letters and papers might give you some ideas for a story," Sarah continued.

I helped Sarah load the rocker into her vehicle. Giving her a kiss on her cheek, I wiped a tear away. "She's with Dad now. You know that she's happy, Sis," I said.

Dad had been the one and only love in Mom's life. His life had been cut short. He died when a roll of steel broke loose and crushed him in a steel-rolling mill accident. Her love for him endured to the end. She never remarried. Sarah was a product of that love, born after his death.

After my sister drove off in her minivan to her home in Wexford, I returned to Mom's apartment to gather the things I had claimed. I looked around. The room felt so empty. The life force fled the apartment with Mom's passing. I placed the family Bible inside the cardboard box with Mom's papers and folded the quilt over the top. Dad's ring was in my pocket. I turned off the lights as I left.

Missing

Stopping at the Super's basement apartment, I returned the keys to Mom's apartment. "The Salvation Army will be stopping by later today to take the few pieces of furniture. Would you be available to let them in?"

"That's no problem, Tommy. I'm sorry about your mom. She was a great woman," he said offering his condolences, then took the key.

"Thanks, Frank," I said. Picking up the box, I left the building.

※

After a not-so-restful night of sleep, I lifted the battered bourbon carton to one of the chairs at my kitchen table, then started a pot of coffee. Pulling a pad and pen from my junk drawer, I laid them on the table. I leaned against the countertop waiting for my coffee to brew.

A slow eddy of lemony Pine-Sol softly filtered into my kitchen to compete with the aroma of the coffee. I knew that Uncle Aidan was hovering near, waiting to see what was in the box and wanting to see if it held clues that would help me unravel John's disappearance.

John, my younger brother, disappeared nearly fifty years ago from the front yard of our Munhall home. The box of papers intensified my desire to look for John. The incident had been investigated by the Pittsburgh city police, but they had come up empty. His disappearance had never been solved.

"John's disappearance hit the whole family hard, Tommy. I could barely put two words together. As a police reporter it was my job, but there weren't many clues and none of them panned out."

It still bothers me, Uncle. That's why I have to find out what happened to him.

The detectives finally relegated John to the cold case files when they came to the decision that it was a random crime. They had never discovered a motive. There was never a ransom note, not that our family could have paid it. We weren't rich. They never found his body and our family had been in limbo ever since, not knowing what had happened to him.

The police may have relegated Johnny's disappearance to a cold case, but Mom never did. Johnny was always on her mind.

The contents of the cardboard box were a mystery. I didn't know what to expect. Packed inside the carton were my mother's private thoughts. I was almost afraid to start, but soon I realized that it was necessary.

My brother's disappearance was a case that the investigators had stopped working on long ago. I hadn't able to pursue it with any consistency on my own. While I was still a cop, I'd been kept busy on heavy caseloads for the city and at the same time trying to salvage my faltering marriage. Now that I'd retired from the police force and my wife was an ex, I had the time, but the catalyst that caused me to turn my full attention to my brother's case was my mother's death.

When the coffee was ready, I poured a cup. It was time to tackle the contents of the box. I was on edge just thinking about the things I might find inside. At the same time, my desire to know what it contained cast its spell on me.

Settling my bottom onto the chrome legged chair, I lifted the lid of the bourbon box beside me. I took the Bible out and placed it on the table. Tucked inside its pages were snapshots of Dad and Mom, a few of Johnny, some photos of Sarah and of me. There was one of Mom, Dad, me, and Johnny and one of Mom with Sarah, Johnny, and me. I didn't notice any clues on them about the disappearance of John, only the dates on the photos. Mom hadn't written anything on the reverse sides of the pictures.

"*You all were a nice family,*" Uncle LeClerc said. "*You'll need to make copies of them for Sarah.*"

Thanks, Unc. I know.

Reaching into the box, I retrieved a scrapbook. The odor of bleach grew stronger. Aidan moved much closer. Under the scrapbook, several stacks of letters, many discolored by age, were gathered into neat bundles by ribbons. A few of the bundles had my father's name on them and the others had John's name on them.

"*Look at all of those letters,*" Aidan said. "*Your mom wrote and saved them all these years. They must have meant a lot to her. I can tell she really loved you all.*"

Yeah, Uncle, I know she did. I remember all of the little things that she did for us even though money was always tight. My mouth went dry. I took a sip of the coffee. Recently, Aidan was being more subtle with the odors of his cleaning supplies. I was able to enjoy the flavor of my coffee and my food.

The old green scrapbook was held together in places with yellowing strips of cellophane tape. Water spots covered the raised design of its surface.

"*Those are from her tears,*" Uncle Aidan said, "*your mother's tears.*"

Tenderly, I ran my hand over the surface. I felt the hairs on the back of my neck rise. With so many tearstains on the outside, I just knew that there would be so much sadness bound between its worn velvet covers.

Am I ready for this? I wondered. Big, tough cop that I was, I wasn't sure that I could handle it.

Taking another sip of coffee to bolster my flagging confidence, I opened to the front page. A clipping from the *Pittsburgh Post-Gazette* announced the accident at the Confluence Steel Plant that had crushed my father.

Confluence Steel Accident Kills One, Injures Three Others

In a bizarre accident, one man was crushed and three others were injured at the Confluence Steel Works when chains lifting a roll of steel broke, allowing the mass of metal to fall down on them. James Minerd was directly below. He was killed instantly. The injured were rescued and sent to near-by hospitals.

Two of the men were seriously injured and are not expected to survive. The plant manager said, "There is an ongoing investigation of the incident." He would give no further details at this time.

Below the article, several yellowed newspaper photographs were taped in the scrapbook of the Confluence Plant and the accident site. The cellophane tape had darkened with age and barely held the pictures to the page.

My throat constricted. It was the first time that I'd seen this article. I knew that my dad had died, I even knew the facts. But there it was, hitting me full in the face, written down, and printed in black on the yellowed page. Each word was difficult and painful for me to read.

Aidan was close. The subtle scent of lemon changed to one of lavender Lysol and it enveloped me. It was as close to giving me comfort as he was able.

Thanks, Uncle Aidan.

I appreciated the kindness of his gesture, as I took in the enormity of the stark pronouncement. It wasn't a clue to find my brother, but it gave me insight into my past. The next page held my father's obituary and the announcement from the funeral home. I moved on before I could become maudlin and abandon the scrapbook project altogether. I needed to see what Mom had tucked away on the rest of the pages.

There were photographs of Nana and Pap, some of John and me and some of Sarah right after her birth. Her photo was taped next to her birth announcement. I can only imagine my mom's jumbled emotions at Sarah's birth; the joy of the birth so close on the heels of tragedy. Although she'd lost my father, she had a piece of him reborn in Sarah.

On the next page was the face of my brother staring back at me from the article Mom had clipped from the paper. Above the photo the heading read:

Child Goes Missing

John Minerd, 3, disappeared from his yard at his Munhall home. He has sandy blond hair, green eyes, is twenty-eight inches tall and weighs forty-eight pounds. Pittsburgh police are investigating. They ask that anyone with information about the incident contact them at 412-555-5505.

I was too young then to do anything about my brother's disappearance, but now that I was old enough, inquisitive enough, and had enough time to pursue this cold case, I could possibly do something to find out what had happened to him.

I fear the worst, Uncle Aidan, but I still need to know what happened to him. It was my fault that John went missing.

A small puff of Pine-Sol whisked past my nostrils. Aidan said, "You need to look back, Tommy. There are clues for you there. You'll be able to use them to find other things that will help you."

I need to pull his file at the police station, too.

Being a retired Pittsburgh cop, I still had some perks that would allow me to review the information that the cops had discovered with their investigation—witnesses, clues, and dead end trails. It should limit the amount of repeat work that I would have to do.

I needed to eat breakfast before I decided to go through any more information. Not feeling like eating my own cooking, I headed for P's Café.

Walking along the street just outside of my apartment, my uncle said, *"What is that fantastic smell?"*

I replied sarcastically, *I didn't know that you could smell anything with all of your cleaning supplies. All I can smell is the Pine-Sol cloud that follows you around.*

"That's not fair. You know what I think about germs," Aidan said. *"I love the fragrance of that fresh baking bread. Can't you smell it?"*

The breeze shifted. The wonderful yeasty aroma of baking bread overrode the Pine-Sol. I made a slight detour from my walk to P's Café, following my nose.

Around the corner, I found that a new bakery had opened. Over the window and door of the storefront, a green and white striped sign stated in tall, black lettering, "Brickle's Bakery." In the window, a hand lettered sign announced, breads, buns, and pies. I stood outside for only a few seconds before the escaping aromas seduced me to step inside.

As I entered, I cautioned, *Aidan, please stay back and let me enjoy this.* I breathed deeply, savoring the bouquet of baked goods.

A brass bell attached to a curved black metal arm was clipped to the top of the old-fashioned, heavy glass and wood door. It jangled, announcing my entrance. The shop consisted of a narrow sales area lined with long wood and glass display cases.

Missing

From the back room came a slender gray haired lady with flour on her hands. She carried a large tray of cinnamon buns. When she first caught sight of me, she almost dropped the tray. Her pallor faded and nearly matched the smear of flour on her cheek.

As she stood there, the savory cinnamon aroma filled the sales room. Finally she asked, "May I help you?" Shakily, she slid the tray of sticky buns into the case.

"If your baked goods taste half as good as they smell, I'm in for a treat. Those buns helped me make up my mind on what I wanted. How much are a half dozen?" I said as I pointed to the tray.

She gave a weak chuckle, "Half dozen would be six dollars. And they better be good. I've been baking for fifty-eight years." Her badge announced her as Margie Brickle.

"Your business is new in the neighborhood. I can't remember being drawn here by the enticing aroma of fresh bread before."

"Me and my son, David, lost our lease on the building that we were renting on the North Side and we found this place. The old building was getting too big for me and David since my husband died. This is a bit smaller, but that makes it easier for me. I'm not as young as I used to be."

"*Everything smells so good,*" Aidan said. "*But before you buy anything, let me check out the kitchen.*" The small cloud of Pine-Sol left the room.

At least you're keeping control on the amounts of your cleaning fluids.

Margie washed her hands and donned plastic gloves before she placed six of the steaming, gooey cinnamon buns into the folded box on the waxed paper lining.

She washed her hands and put on gloves, Uncle Aidan.

Her white dress and apron were clean. *That should make you happy, Aidan.* I decided to share the buns with Vera and Ed at the café with enough left over for a late night snack and for breakfast the next morning.

"I have a friend who runs a café a few blocks away. With your bakery so close, she may want to order from you. I'm not sure where she buys her baked goods now, but they can't be fresher than if she bought them from your bakery. I'll have her call you."

She rang the sales on an old key-punch cash register. Margie wrote the phone number for the bakery on the top of the box. I left the shop with the bottom of the container warm on my hands.

"They must be fresh," Aidan said.

These rolls will have to taste good if I can still smell the cinnamon over your Pine-Sol, Uncle.

He didn't say a word; I knew he was pouting.

I walked into the café just as Vera poured Ed's coffee to complete his breakfast.

Ed looked over his shoulder as the bells on a red cord that hung from the doorknob announced my entrance.

"Hey, Tommy," Ed called. "Pull up a stool."

Vera said, "Hi, Tommy." Then asked, "What can I get you?"

"Just some coffee for now. I brought something to share with yinzs," I replied.

Before I opened the box, Vera had a cup of joe on the counter in front of me. When I lifted the lid, the cinnamon smell welled out.

Stay away, Aidan. I want to savor every bite.

"Those smell great," Vera said. She turned around, reaching for a saucer.

"Grab three, one for each of us."

When Vera turned back around she had three saucers, forks, and a large knife. Soon, each of us had our mouths filled with the sticky buns and smiles stuck on our faces.

"There's a new bakery just down the street. You may want to check their prices, Vera. Mrs. Brickle may be able to supply your café. Their shop's so close. If the price is right, the buns would certainly be fresh." I traded the bakery box for a doggy bag, so Vera would have the bakery's phone number.

※

Back at my apartment, I dropped off the remainder of my rolls, then grabbed my pad and pen. I headed to the police station while there was a good chance that my friend, Sergeant Duggan was on duty. We had a long history together coming up through the ranks. I figured that if anyone could help me get a look at that cold case file, he could.

I was in luck. Sergeant Duggan was at the front desk. He looked up as I entered, "Hey, Tommy, how are you doing? I heard your mom passed away. Sorry to hear."

"Thanks, Sarge. It's been rough the past few weeks, but I'm doing okay."

"What brought you in today?"

"I'm doing a follow up on a cold case. I need you to help me have a look-see at the file."

"What was the case?" Duggan asked.

"It's the case of my missing brother, John."

"When was that Tommy?"

"October 12, 1961."

"I'll need to get clearance from the Captain, but I think I can swing it." The sergeant reached for the phone and punched a button. "Captain Emerick, this is Duggan at the front desk. I got Tommy Two Shoes here. He wants to review one of our cold cases that he's working on. It's about John, his missing brother."

Sarge paused and listened. "Yeah, that's right, Tommy Two Shoes."

Another pause, then, "Okay, thanks, Cap." He hung up the phone. "You got his blessing. I just have to write a note to Laverne in the file room. She'll need it for her files."

"Thanks, Sarge," I said as he handed me the note.

I hurried down the stairs to the basement and entered the file room. When Laverne caught sight of me she hurried across the floor from her desk and crushed me in a bear hug. "Tommy, you haven't changed one bit." She bellowed in my ear loud enough to shatter my eardrums.

Laverne was five three, two hundred pounds, black, wavy hair, and dark brown eyes that peered from behind large framed glasses with thick lenses. Her skin looked like smooth brown velvet even though she was creeping upon retirement age. She looked a full five years younger.

"Laverne, you get more beautiful and younger looking every time I see you."

I could smell Pine-Sol. I wasn't sure whether I was about to find a clue or whether someone had started to clean somewhere in the basement.

Laverne gave me a playful punch and giggled, saying, "Go on, you sweet talker, you. Duggan called. I have your file on the table over there. I do need that note though."

A small battered and scarred wooden table had finally worked its way through the department until it had been relegated to this spot in the basement. The table had been placed directly under an overhead hanging light. Its surface was large enough to spread out the files into several stacks and still have room for my legal pad.

After I handed her the note, I said, "Laverne, you're a darling. Thanks." I made my way to the table, then pulled out the old wooden chair. The chair grated on the painted concrete floor.

The smell of Lysol merged with the odor of Pine-Sol. Aidan said, *"Lift the chair, Tommy. Don't slide it. You'll scuff the paint and I can't stand to hear that noise. You need to start looking back."*

What do you think I'm doing, Uncle Aidan?

I separated the information into piles—photos, interviews, clues, and fingerprints. I began by looking at the photographs of the front yard of our old home before we moved in with Nana and Pappy.

"So that's where it happened," Aidan spoke softly in my ear. A faint bleach odor sneaked up on me. As a former police reporter, he showed extra interest.

Yes.

The lump in my throat wouldn't allow me to say any more.

I lifted a photo from the pile and stared at it. The photo stirred a myriad of memories. They pushed in on me with stunning impact. The pleasures of a childhood playtime collided with the horror, fear, and confusion that occurred with the disappearance of my brother coming so close to the shadow cast by my dad's death.

The wellspring of emotions that had been bottled up over the years rushed out in torrents with the power of a hurricane. I sat there, stunned into immobility. My eyes stared unseeing through a tidal wave of tears.

The aroma of linen-scented bleach grew stronger. Uncle Aidan was close. I could almost feel his comforting hand as he leaned over my shoulder.

Laverne placed a steaming cup of strong, black coffee at my

elbow. It drew me out of my mind numbing emotional trance. "I thought some coffee would help keep you awake while you're going over the files."

I pulled my handkerchief out of my pocket and blew my nose, wiping my eyes at the same time.

"Thanks, Laverne. You're so thoughtful." My voice was still husky with emotion.

"I remembered while you worked here, you always enjoyed your coffee," Laverne said. "And I just made a fresh pot."

She turned and went back to work at her desk. I returned to the files, studying the multiple photos that had been taken of our yard from several different angles. There was one photo that caused the lump in my throat to return. Spread out on the sidewalk were the scattered remains of a sandwich.

"Just like those photos, you'll have to look at the clues from different views to find out what happened to your brother. Who knows where it will lead. It's been such a long time."

I have to try, I shared my thoughts with Aidan. *I'm ashamed that it's taken me this long to do something.*

I was definitely embarrassed that it took the death of my mom to spur me into action. The thoughts that it had been my fault over the years were almost too heavy to bear.

Shaking off those feelings, I went to work reading and rereading every statement, combing through each interview with neighbors, witnesses, and each possible clue. Gleaning every possibility from the records consumed me. I copied names and phone numbers, as well as anything I thought might be pertinent.

When I looked up, Laverne's desk was empty. She'd gone. I'd emptied the pot of coffee and my bladder was full. I gathered the papers from the file and placed it in the basket on Laverne's desk. The note I put on top said, simply, "Thanks for the coffee. Tommy."

I picked up my pad of notes and pen, then hurried to the nearest bathroom.

※

Back at my apartment, I went over the information I'd gathered. The two detectives who'd caught the investigation had died, but from their report, I had gleaned the names of the neighbors and the statements that they'd given. There were phone numbers, but most would have been changed or disconnected. I needed to find out who was still alive and where they were, to see if they'd remembered anything more over the intervening years. Finding anyone with more information would be a long shot, but I had nothing else to try.

Sitting at my kitchen table, I noticed the letters nestled in my mom's box. There were envelopes addressed to my dad that were tied with red ribbons, his favorite color, and my brother's, bound with his favorite, green. Mom paid attention to detail and showed them the love she couldn't give them in person. I wasn't ready to tackle that sensitive quagmire yet. Choked with emotion, I could hardly breathe.

"*She really loved you all. Look at her thoughtfulness,*" Aidan comforted.

I closed the lid and turned my attention to the information I'd gathered from the cold case file.

"*Whew, it's going to be a big job. You'll have to check out each name and track them down. Do a follow up, check obituaries, and find the people who've moved away,*" Uncle LeClerc said as he appeared in a thin cloud of lemon Lysol.

Thanks for toning back on the Lysol smell. I like to know when you're around, but I don't want to be suffocated. It's a fairly long list of people, but looking at some of the ages, I'd be surprised if any of them would still be still alive.

I turned on my computer and began the search. Many of them had been in their sixties seventies at the time of the crime. I was right. Most of them were found listed in the obituaries. I crossed them off, one by one. Several names remained who'd moved out of state and a few other ones that didn't appear in the obituaries or anywhere else.

Now, came the hard part—tracking those missing names down. Some folks lived locally, but there had been no answers on their phones. Finally, I reached a man who still lived in the house across the street from our old home. Mr. Tillman and his wife had been a young couple who lived in the neighborhood when John disappeared from our widowed mom.

Three rings before a male voice answered, "Hello."

"Mr. Tillman?"

"Yes."

"This is Tommy Minerd. I was the boy who used to live across the street from you when my brother, John, went missing."

"Oh, hi, Tommy. What can I do for you?" Mr. Tillman asked.

"To make a long story short, I'm a retired cop and I'm trying to find out what happened to John all those years ago. I'm reopening the cold case and was wondering if I would be able to stop by and talk to you?"

"You know where I live. Stop by anytime, Tommy."

I glanced at my watch. "I'll stop by in about an hour if that's okay."

"Sure, Tommy, I'll be waiting."

Missing

※

I hurried from my apartment to catch the bus. The seductive scent of cinnamon reached out, luring me aside into Brickle's Bakery. I was greeted by the bell and Margie Brickle. "Hi, what can I get for you today?"

"I'd like another half dozen of those cinnamon rolls. You've made me an addict, I believe."

She studied my face before saying, "I'm sorry David isn't here. I wanted him to meet you." She busied herself, packaging the rolls. "He comes in later in the day to help me clean and close up shop after he makes his deliveries."

I didn't have time to make small talk. I had a bus to catch. Snatching up the box, I made a bee line to the stop on the corner. Initially, I got an angry look when I wedged into a bus seat between two women. They hugged their large purses more tightly on their laps. Every once in a while, one of the other passengers would glance hungrily at the box of goodies I held.

I climbed off the bus at the end of Dill Avenue. I wanted to walk through the neighborhood to get a feel for any changes. Some homes had been torn down, some were remodeled, and some looked as though they'd never changed. Here and there, some had been divided into apartments.

"You're almost home," Uncle Aidan murmured as the scent of lemon Lysol wafted past me.

It was odd how although some things had changed, the street still had the same feel. As I grew nearer, it was almost as though all of those years were being peeled away. I felt myself grow younger as I walked nearer the house where I'd once lived. Stopping on the sidewalk, I stared. I was a five year old kid again. The fear that I'd felt when I'd initially found my brother missing returned. It was like a sucker punch in the gut.

The house had been painted, there were new windows, and the yard had been landscaped. The old turkey wire fence was changed unto a chest high, twisted wire fence with a locking gate. The thick hedge was gone, but it was our house.

Standing frozen on the walkway, I was a child, thrown back to that day fifty years ago.

I had just finished my Islay's chipped-chopped ham sandwich with Heinz ketchup. John sat on the stoop still eating his. I wanted more orange-aide drink. I ran back into the house for a refill. When I came back outside, John was gone. All that was left were the remnants of his sandwich scattered on the ground.

"Keep looking back," Aidan said.

From the recesses of my mind, I heard myself call, "Mo-o-o-o-m!" My voice was sharp, edged with panic. I was caught—unable to move—trapped at that very instant in my life.

"Tommy?" a male voice called.

I turned. It was Mr. Tillman. He was sitting on the swing of his front porch. He returned my wave and nodded.

The Lysol smell grew stronger. *"I hope that he's more talkative than that,"* Aidan said.

Crossing the street, I ambled up Tillman's walkway. "Mr. Tillman."

"Yaa-up," came the answer. "Come on up." He rose from the swing. "I have some coffee on."

As I climbed the steps, I said, "I have cinnamon rolls for us, too." I held the box up for him to see.

I followed him across the porch, through the screened door, and down a short hallway into a kitchen that hadn't changed since the 1960s. On the wall, hung a clock shaped like a teapot. The floor was gray linoleum with royal blue Congoleum that ran half way up the wall. Bent chrome legged chairs surrounded a red Formica topped kitchen table.

"Have a seat," Mr. Tillman said, pointing to a chair. "What do you like in your coffee?"

"I take it black, thanks." Two thick mugs of steaming joe appeared on the table. He turned back to a cupboard and fetched two pale green Melmac saucers with knives and forks, then sat down across from me. I used my knife to separate the buns and lift one out for each of us. After his first sip of coffee, he asked, "What can I help you with?"

"I'm trying to turn up new clues about my brother John."

"He's the kid who disappeared from across the street about fifty years ago."

"Right, I'm a retired cop now. I need to find out what happened to him. I wanted to ask if you remembered anything new over the years."

He paused for a second, then took another sip of his coffee. "I did think of something that I'd seen. The cops who investigated said they'd be back. When they didn't return, I forgot all about it."

A spark of hope struck a light in my heart at his recollection. I pulled my pad and pen out of my shirt pocket. "What was it that you remembered, Mr. Tillman?" I had to wait as he finished chewing a bite of the roll.

When he spoke, he remarked, "That's a great cinnamon roll. I haven't had anything this good since my Marilyn died." He paused again before saying, "What I remembered was a younger man walking up and down the street in front of your house for several weeks before your brother went missing. The man would always look into your yard, especially when you and your brother were outside playing."

"Can you describe him?"

Mr. Tillman leaned back in his chair. It creaked under his weight. "I didn't see him the morning your brother disappeared, but the man that I saw earlier was a white guy, in his early twenties, slender, with short brown hair, and was wearing white trousers and a white T-shirt. I couldn't see the color of his eyes, but he would walk up the street, turn, and walk back down. He came back every couple of days to walk along the street. After your brother went missing, I never saw him again. The one thing I do remember is he had a large red heart tattoo on his left forearm. The heart had some kind of an 'M' name in it, Mary, Marie, something like that. I remembered that because it was the same first letter as in Marilyn's name."

"The police never got this information?"

"That's right. They never came back."

He had nothing else to offer, so we sat and talked. He told me some stories about my dad as we finished our snacks and coffee.

"It's not much, but it's a new start. It will give us a picture of a possible male suspect to look for," Uncle Aidan said.

I pushed the box of remaining cinnamon rolls across the table and said, "Thanks for your help, Mr. Tillman, please take the rest of these rolls. I brought them to share."

I could tell by the sparkle in his eyes that I'd made a new friend. "Thanks." He reached across the table to shake my hand. We rose and walked to the front door. "If there is anything else I can do for you, let me know," he said. The spring on the screen door groaned open as I left.

Walking to the bus stop, something I'd seen began to niggle at my brain. But what was it and where had I seen it? Each time I reached for it, it danced seductively just beyond my consciousness.

It slipped away, elusive and indistinct.

I climbed onto the bus, finally deciding to let the intangible wisp stay in the darkness. Since I couldn't put my hands on it, I let it lay. There was no use worrying about it until it came out into the light on its own.

※

I spent the next few days searching for the few people that I hadn't yet crossed off the list of those who'd been interviewed by the police. I found a few more that were at home and questioned them over the phone. I didn't find any more clues, although I did coincidentally find a woman who had babysat for me and my brother as kids. She wished me the best of luck when she found out that I was looking for John.

My eyes got tired and I was stressed. I put aside my pad and pen. I needed to relax and stop thinking about the case. Sometimes as a cop, I found out that if I put down what I was working on, my brain would sort things out.

I headed toward P's Café to grab a bite to eat. I caught a whiff of freshly baked goods from Brickle's, but it disappeared behind a barrage of the piney Pine-Sol odor. *"You're getting closer. Just don't be discouraged. This has remained unsolved for fifty years, Tommy. You can't expect to solve it in a couple of days,"* Aidan said.

I walked into P's and grabbed a stool. I still chose to sit on one of those lumpy stools. Once I got into a habit, it was hard for me to break. It took a rap on the head to get me move—once.

Vera said, "Thanks, Tommy," as she slid a steaming cup of java in front of me.

"Thanks for what?" I asked.

"Your tip on the new bakery. I'm buying my buns from

them now. They're fresher and I save a dollar on each dozen. I'm buying a few cinnamon buns, too. I've added them to my breakfast menu. Now people are stopping by for the cinnamon rolls and coffee to go. You just missed the delivery guy. He left a few minutes ago. I was busy and barely had time to take the rolls and pay him. I didn't get to meet him. Are you making any headway finding your brother?"

Seeing her smile had always warmed my heart. "Just inching along."

"You're an old softie, Tommy," Aidan said out of a soft nebulous haze of lemon Lysol. *"You need to keep looking back."*

Uncle Aidan, you are much older than me, and I'm doing my best to look back.

"Tommy, I'm a ghost. I won't get any older than I am now," Aidan chuckled.

We reached an understanding. I would pay more attention to what my uncle said and he would tone down the potency of his arrivals.

You're sounding like a broken record. Look back. Look back. I've been doing my best, Uncle Aidan. I'm reviewing everything that I can get my hands on.

"You just need to look in the right spot. If you would start looking from an opposite point of view, you might find the key you need," LeClerc said.

That's easy for you to say, Uncle Aidan. I've been trying to sort out fifty years of stale clues and follow an ice cold trail. It's not easy for me. You need to be more specific. You're driving me crazy.

"I'm sorry, Tommy. Give me time and I'll help you sort things out. I'll direct you and get you in the right frame of mind," Uncle Aidan said.

More clues, I'm sure. I pulled my notebook out and wrote

them down so I'd be sure I remember them for later.

Vera said, "I can't imagine what it would be like to have someone missing for fifty years. I almost died when Ed was missing for just a couple of days." Reaching across the counter, she covered my hand with hers. At one time, that gesture would have set my heart racing, but now that she was married and I was dating Cora, it was only a soothing balm and a welcomed gesture. "Thanks for finding him for me."

※

Sitting at my kitchen table, I decided it was time to look at a few of the letters my mom had written. Just possibly, there could be a clue hidden in them.

Dear Jimmy,

It grieves me to tell you this, but our little Johnny is missing. The boys were playing in the yard when Johnny disappeared. The police have been here and gone. Reporters have been knocking on our door all day long. I had to go to your parent's house to get rid of them.

I don't know what to do. Waiting to hear anything about Johnny is so hard. I jump each time the phone rings. I just want to scream. I want him to be found. Why don't the police call? I don't know where my baby boy is.

Time has gone by so slowly. Each day seems to last for an eternity. I don't know what has happened to Johnny. He's not here and I can't watch over him. I'll have to ask you to do that for me, James.

> *We moved in with your mom and dad. Each day seems so long. Nothing seems the same or any easier without you. I just wanted you to know that I still love you and miss you so much. I will always love you.*
>
> *Your loving wife,*
> *Rebecca*

I sucked in my breath. Mom hadn't blamed me for Johnny's disappearance. The thoughts of her blaming me had haunted me for fifty years. It was a subject that we'd never breached. I was stunned, then relieved. Much of the burden lifted.

The letters had been written at least one per year. Mom shared her love in each word, writing what was in her heart and what had happened through the year. She told Dad about Sarah and me growing up and what we were doing. Most of the letters were similar. I was finding nothing in the letters that would help solve the disappearance of Johnny.

The theme of each letter expressed her extreme loneliness. There was little hope left in the letters, only the love she had for Sarah and me. I skipped to the last letter that she'd written Dad.

Dear Jimmy,

> *I am so very weary and haven't been feeling well for years. I feel so stretched out. I haven't told the kids. They're all grown now. I feel so alone. Sometimes, the memories of you press so close, I can hardly breathe. Life has become so oppressive and burdensome. I am not sure how much longer I can carry on. This may be the last letter until I join you my love. My broken heart has never mended. I fear it will never heal until I am re-united with you.*
>
> *All my love; your faithful wife,*
> *Rebecca*

She'd been sick and hadn't told us. It was the last note that Mom ever wrote to Dad.

I read through the letters that Mom had written to Johnny. They were much like the ones she'd written to Dad. She shared her love and kept Johnny updated on the things that were happening with our family.

I need a break.

Re-bundled, I plopped the letters back into the box. A puff of dust rose out of the box.

"Be careful of all that dust," LeClerc coughed. An odor of Pine-Sol quickly filled the air. *"There has to be mold in that dust, too. Be more careful, Nephew. You need to look back; on all sides of the information that you already have gone through, before you go searching elsewhere."*

Not now, Uncle. I'm not in the mood. I was feeling down and depressed after reading my mom's letters. *What do you think I've been trying to do?*

"Don't forget to wash your hands."

※

When I climbed out of the sagging seat of my recliner after a nap, I walked into the kitchen and sat at the table. I glanced into the box. Seeing those letters bound in green ribbons still brought back the feelings that I was somehow responsible for John going missing.

"It had to be hard for you bearing that burden all these years. You were just a kid yourself, but your mom didn't blame you," Aidan said. Mists of lavender Lysol seeped into the kitchen. *"You can't continue to carry it anymore."*

I put my head down on the table and bawled. All of those

emotions that had built up over fifty years came rushing out.

I was looking through the eyes of five years old again, sitting on the porch stoop. Mom ran from the house and began to search frantically. Her screams, "Johnny! Johnny! JOHNNY!" echoed in my ears and her voice still resounded in my brain. I was back on the porch, staring down at my navy blue Keds and the drying crusts of my brother's sandwich not knowing what else to do.

Mr. Tillman rushed across the street. He made the phone call to the police, then joined the other neighbors in scouring the neighborhood for Johnny.

Two patrolmen arrived. After settling Mom down, they questioned her. Once the cops got a description and a photo of John, they called in a missing child report. Other policemen joined the search. Mom continued to answer the two patrolmen's questions. Once they'd left, she broke down again as she sat on the living room couch. Her sobbing replayed, over and over again in my mind. I stood unnoticed, forgotten, taking it all in.

The aroma of lavender Lysol surrounded me. I lifted my head. The Lysol smell still lingered. It was a touch of comfort. *Thanks, Uncle Aidan. You've become a good friend to me.*

Slowly, I plodded through each word Mom had written. My eyes were tired, but I decided to finish by reading the last letter. It was the final correspondence Mom had written to John. The level of lavender intensified. I paused. I was almost afraid to open the envelope.

Dear Johnny,

I've been sick for quite some time and I've given up hope of ever seeing you again. I haven't said anything to your brother and sister. They'd press me to search for cures and miracles, but I am worn out. Life has made too many demands on me. I can't handle anymore. I don't plan to do anything to myself, but I don't want to hold on any longer.

I'm sure that you have grown to be a big, handsome man like your brother by now. I can only wonder what you've done with your life, whether you've married, and whether you've given me any grandchildren.

I pray that one day you will read my words. I can't accept the thought that you're not alive. Wherever you are and whatever you are doing, I want you to know that I love you now and forever.

All my love,

Mom

"You need to look back. You'll never get the full picture of what happened to your brother until you look back." A lemon bleach cloud filled my kitchen.

I was getting tired of hearing Uncle LeClerc say the same thing. His words angered me and kept me from sinking into a pit of despair.

I heard you, Aidan, and I am trying. I don't know what else to do.

Glancing at my watch, I noticed that it was nearly two a.m. Heading to my bedroom, I decided to catch a few hours of sleep before hoofing it to the bakery for another order of cinnamon rolls. I fell asleep dreaming of sticky buns.

※

I woke, feeling groggy. *The lack of sleep and too much caffeine. I can't believe I just said I'd had too much coffee.*

"That's definitely one for the record books," LeClerc said. His chuckle told me that he wasn't suffering from our late night session.

Freshly showered, I felt better and walked to Brickle's Bakery. After a few minutes, I entered the bake shop. The luscious, yeasty aroma of freshly baked breads surrounded me. "Good morning, Mrs. Brickle. I couldn't resist stopping by for your cinnamon rolls."

"They're coming out of the oven now. Give me a few minutes and you'll have some of the freshest rolls you've ever eaten." She disappeared into the back room.

I wandered around the salesroom. There were several black and white photos on the walls. I'd noticed them before, but never looked to see what they were. I moved closer. The fragrance of Pine-Sol crept into the bakery and mingled with the savory smells of fresh bread. Aidan was close. The photo that I was looking at was one of an old bakery with a younger Mrs. Brickle holding a baby in her arms. The date on the photo was 1958. A young man stood at her side.

A noise behind me let me know that Margie had returned. The cinnamon aroma intensified, covering Aidan's Pine-Sol smell. Margie emerged from the back room.

"That photo was of our family at the old bakery," Mrs. Brickle said as she hoisted the large tray of sticky buns into the slots of the glass display case. She separated a half dozen of the rolls and placed them in a box.

I paid for the treats, then hurried home. The aroma filled the stairway as I climbed the steps to my apartment. I turned the coffee pot on and stared out the window at pigeon droppings as I waited. The feeling that I'd seen or heard something important grew stronger, but what was it?

I soon had coffee to go with my breakfast. Sitting in my kitchen, I saw that my mom's scrapbook was still sitting at one side of the table.

"You really need to look back. You won't find out what happened until you can see the whole picture," Aidan said.

I decided to flip through the clippings while I ate. Maybe, I'd missed something. I opened the book to the first page. The old cellophane tape finally gave up the ghost. One of the clippings fluttered onto the floor. When I leaned over to pick it up, I saw the name of David Brickle. It was an article on the back of my dad's obituary.

David Brickle was the name of Margie Brickle's son from the bakery. The article stated that child had died from an accident at the family home.

"*You finally looked at the back,*" Uncle Aidan said. "*You're getting more of the picture now. Why didn't you look sooner?*"

Why couldn't you be more clear? I was so upset that I shook the obituary at Aidan. *I've been running all over town, looking for clues and I had this one right under my nose all the time.* David and my brother John were almost the same age.

The thought that had been so elusive came into focus. The man wearing white clothing that Mr. Tillman had described looked like the man in the photo I'd seen in Margie's bakery.

I had to get another look at that photo hanging on the bakery wall, but I decided to wait. From what Margie said, David was usually in the bakery around noon. I'd waited for fifty years; another few hours wouldn't mean much. I wanted to meet him.

I had to be sure of my facts. Using the computer, I did a thorough search. I couldn't find any more children born to Margie Brickle.

While I waited, I copied and studied all of LeClerc's clues. Ninety percent of them were, "Look back." It had a double meaning that I kept missing. His clues described back, as in time and back, as on the flipside of the obituary. All the other clues that I'd found pointed to the same conclusion. David was John.

※

The bell over the bakery door chimed as I entered. I started across the sales floor to get a better look at the photo when a male voice called from the back room, "Be with you in a minute."

"Okay," I called back.

My heart was pounding in my chest. I was about to meet this man, David, and I hoped, my brother John.

I stared at the young man dressed in white pictured in the photograph. Prominently on the left forearm was the heart tattoo with the name Margie through it. Unless this was a major coincidence, I was about to learn the truth. If my assumption was correct, I was about to meet my missing brother. My stomach lurched and suddenly it filled with butterflies.

I heard steps behind me. I swallowed. "That's Mom and Dad with me," the male voice said.

I paused, then turned around. I felt as though I was looking into a mirror. I saw a slightly younger version of myself.

"How can I help...," the voice faltered. I was sure that David saw the resemblance as quickly as I had. He had to have noticed the similarity of our size, hair color, and facial features.

A series of questions hit me. How should I approach him? What should I say to him? I felt my throat constrict and my mouth dried, but I managed to say, "You must be David." I extended my hand. "Your mom has said so much about you."

I watched as he studied me, struggling to find a place in his memory for my familiar looking face. The silence was awkward.

But what else could it be? Two young men that would have

the same name, age, and the same parent's names, there was no other way that it made any sense. This wasn't another Brickle child named David. It was impossible.

Where should I go now? What should I do next? Everything I'd discovered was circumstantial. How could I prove or disprove that David was actually my missing brother Johnny? At the moment, they were just a chain of coincidences.

There was only one way to prove it—DNA, but that would do little more than satisfy my curiosity. Was it worth it to destroy my brother, John/David's life? What would it accomplish? I was in a quandary. There was only a slight chance that he would remember me, my mom, or Sarah. I was almost one hundred percent sure that he was my brother, but I needed some time to think.

David and I were rooted, staring across the counter at each other, but saying nothing.

"You need to buy something and leave. It will give you time to think or else you need to tell him what you think to be true, right now," Aidan said.

The odor of bleach prodded me to say, "Let me have a loaf of bread." The puzzled look on John/David's face disappeared. He was glad that he had something to keep him busy.

He smiled and said, "Right away, sir."

I paid the bill and left the bake shop. My mind was swirling with the enormity of what had just happened. I wandered home in a daze, guided by the faint smell of Pine-Sol. I had so much to think about. Did Margie know? Did I have the right to destroy the life that David knew? Should I tell Sarah? Mom had died, so the onus and urgency had lessened.

Back at my apartment, I reheated the coffee and made a bologna sandwich from the still warm loaf. I smeared some mustard on the slices of bread. As I chewed my sandwich, my mind continued to chew over all of my options. I needed a face to face meeting with Margie Brickle. I had to have more information and she was the only one with answers.

※

I decided to sleep on it, but it was a restless, broken sleep. I woke with a dull, hangover-like headache. It was nothing that a cup of coffee and a few aspirins couldn't cure. I knew the remedy would work from years of experience on the police department.

I made some toast from the bakery bread and brewed some coffee. Slathering some jam on the toast, I made it my breakfast. Once I was showered, I felt half decent again.

As I stepped out of my apartment, a cloud of Pine-Sol enveloped me. *"What are you going to say to her?"*

Right now, I'm just going to find a time and place where I can sit and talk with Margie Brickle. After that, I'm not sure of what I'm going to do.

"Good morning, Mr. Minerd, more cinnamon buns today?" Mrs. Brickle asked.

"I met David yesterday and I think we need to talk."

Her smile disappeared and she nervously wiped her hands on her apron. I knew then that she'd recognized how closely I resembled her son, David, the day we'd first met. What did she know?

"David will be in at noon. He frees me so I can go to lunch. Would that be okay?"

"Do you know where P's Café is located?"

"Yes, it's just down the street," she answered.

"I'll meet you there at 12:30."

A worried look crossed her face as I turned to leave. I hadn't solved anything, I had just postponed it.

I walked into P's. When Vera saw my face, she automatically slid a cup of joe in front of me, and asked, "What's wrong, Tommy?"

I sighed. How should I answer Vera? It was either tell her everything or nothing. I chose the latter. "I have a meeting later that I'd rather avoid, but I need to get some answers."

"What can I do to help? You've done so much for me, Ed, and my parents, more than anyone could expect." Vera's concern for me was thick in her voice.

"I plan to have the meeting here. I'll need the back table around 12:30 today."

"It's yours even if I don't serve anyone at that table all day long. I'll make sure it's empty when you need it."

"Thanks, I owe you one," I replied.

"You're wrong, Tommy. You've done so much for me. I still owe you, more than you can know. How are you and Cora?"

I was embarrassed. With the search for my brother, I'd been neglecting Cora. I still called and talked to her, but our dates since Mom's funeral were nonexistent. I needed to do something to make it up to her. I flipped open my cell phone and called a local florist.

"This is Better Bouquets. How can I help you?"

"I need a large mixed arrangement, heavy on pink roses. How quickly can you have it delivered to Classi-glass?" I gave her the address.

"I can have it there within the hour," the woman on the other end of the line said.

"On the card, I want it to say, 'Cora, missing our time together, Tommy.'" I gave her my credit card number and hung up.

Back at my apartment, I tried to write down all of the thoughts that I wanted to share with my new-found brother. The letter would be to John. I wanted him to know about his "real" father and mother and that he has a sister and me. I wrote that I was a retired policeman. I shared our sister's name and that he had a nephew, and a niece. I put my pad aside. I couldn't finish it until I had talked to Margie Brickle.

"*Nervous?*" Aidan asked through a subtle aroma of bleach.

I'm as nervous as I have ever been as a cop in a tight spot with a cornered suspect, Uncle Aidan. I know everything points to David being my brother, but I can't be positive about them until I can get the rest of the story from Mrs. Brickle.

※

I entered P's Cafe a few minutes after noon. The back table had a hand printed sign that said, "Reserved." As I started for the table, I heard Vera say, "Coffee, Tommy?"

"You know better than to ask." I heard Vera chuckle. That laugh helped me to relax a bit.

As I sat at the table, I heard Aidan say, *"Your usual spot on the stool will be getting jealous."*

At twelve twenty-five, Margie Brickle walked through the door. She glanced around. Spotting me, she walked back to my table. She sat on the chair opposite me.

Vera appeared with two menus and refilled my coffee cup. She asked Margie, "What can I get you to drink?"

"Just some water," Mrs. Brickle said.

Vera was back with the water and said, "When you're ready to order, just wave."

"Lunch is on me, if you can answer some questions," I said.

I was quiet while Margie studied the menu. She closed it and I waved to Vera. I ordered a burger and fries while Margie ordered a grilled cheese and a salad.

By that time I had pulled out my pad and pen, I'd written several questions that I needed to have answered. I wanted to shock her and keep her off balance. I wanted her to know that I meant business and was here to get answers.

"I'm a cop." I paused to let that slightly skewed fact sink in. "I know that your real son died in 1958. I found his obituary. I did the research and found that you had no more children. Where did David come from?"

Margie looked as though I had slapped her. She closed her eyes and breathed deeply. At first, I wasn't sure that she would answer me. There was a long hesitation as she collected herself, then started to speak slowly, in a low voice. I had to lean forward to hear what she was saying.

"I was giving David a bath. The phone rang. I answered it and must have been away too long. I found David had rolled over and was face down in the tub." She gave a soft sob. "I called for help, but it was too late." A tear rolled down her cheek.

I pulled a napkin from the holder and handed it to her as Vera arrived with our food.

When Vera left, Margie said, "After the funeral, I became more and more depressed until I couldn't get out of bed. My husband was having problems running the bakery alone and watching over me. Harold tried everything, but nothing helped. I refused to see a doctor.

"He began to walk when he had the time. He needed to get away from the problems of the bakery and from me. This went on for weeks. He couldn't stand the pressure anymore. One day he came home with a young boy about the same age that David would have been. The boy said his name was John, but after I called him David for weeks, he accepted it as his name. My bouts of depression left when David began to call me Mom.

"I had no idea what Harold had done until I heard two ladies talking in our bakery. They said they were afraid to let their kids play outside after a boy had been snatched from his yard last month in Munhall. I knew then where Harold had gotten David, but I was feeling better and had grown attached to him. I was his mother, now."

She wiped away another tear. "I knew it was wrong, but I just couldn't..."

"I'm his brother, Tommy and he has a sister, Sarah," I said firmly. I wasn't letting her off the hook, because she shed a few tears. There was no excuse for what she had done.

Dead air hung between us, finally she said, "What are you going to tell him?"

I really didn't know how to answer her. I wasn't sure what I was going to do. How could I answer her when I was so unsure? Leaving my burger untouched, I rose from the table, placed a twenty on the counter in front of Vera, "This is for lunch. I'll be back later," and I left. I headed back toward my apartment. I had a letter to finish and a decision to make.

"You have your answer that you wanted about your brother. He's alive," Aidan said as a fresh linen scent enveloped me. *"Now comes the hard part, making the right decision with this information."*

I know, Uncle Aidan, I know.

Missing

❋

Only vague thoughts of what I wanted to write were coming to mind. I wasn't able to finish the letter yet. I started with a few thoughts on scrap paper, but they weren't what I wanted to say. The crumpled attempts littered the floor beside the trashcan. I gave up writing to watch some television, then finally went to bed.

I spent another restless night, but when I woke, I knew what I wanted to say in the letter and I knew what I was going to do. Grabbing a pen, I finished the information that I wanted to share, telling David his name was really John and he was my brother. I gave him my name and phone number. I did the same with Sarah's name and number.

I put copies of our father's clipping of his accidental death, his obituary, David's obituary, and the story of John's disappearance as well as the letter I'd written, into an envelope. Sealing it, I wrote on the front, David Brickle/John Minerd. I placed it on top of the letters that my mom had written to him. I retied the ribbon and placed them all in a shoebox, securing it with a length of string.

When I entered the bakery, a look of panic crossed Mrs. Brickle's face. I placed the shoebox parcel on the counter in front of her. "This box is filled with letters that our mom wrote to John over the years he was missing. I added a letter telling John about our family and our mother's death. It's up to you to do the right thing."

I turned and walked out of the bakery. I made my way to Vera's and ordered breakfast. While I waited for my meal, I pulled my cell from my pocket and dialed. "Hello, Cora, would you like to see a movie tonight?"

More or Les

My cell phone rang. When I saw the number, I recognized that it was a call from my baby sister, Sarah. A quick blast of lemon scented Lysol swirled around my head.

Okay, Uncle LeClerc, I'm getting your message, loud and clear. Aidan's appearance was always in scented clouds of cleaning supplies. He was in an odd way like the Lone Ranger, but unlike the Lone Ranger, Uncle Aidan would never arrive in a cloud of dust. He hated dust.

"Hey, Sarah," I answered.

"Hi, Tommy." Aidan's sudden arrival became coupled with the worried sound of Sarah's voice. She had a problem that was about to be mine.

Some people say that they can smell trouble coming. With me it was literal. Aidan's repertoire of aromas in his cleaning supply arsenal seemed almost endless. It was only limited by the products on the market. Over the years, I was never sure how Aidan would arrive. One thing I could say, he kept up with new cleaning supplies and their changing aromas.

"What do you need, Sis?"

"How do you know that I'm having a problem?"

"I have my ways." There was no need to share my ace in the hole, Aidan LeClerc. He was our uncle and a ghost who gave clues to me. She wouldn't have believed me, even if I had told her.

"You're almost right, but the problem isn't with me, it's with Sammy."

Sammy was my nephew, Sarah's son.

"His girlfriend, Robin, left him. They're on the outs. Against my advice they've been living together. I told them that unless you're both totally committed to make this work, don't start. But, of course, youthful lusts spoke with a louder voice than a mother's wisdom."

I wondered if she wanted me to be the peacemaker. I hoped not. From my own experience, I understood that sometimes separation was the best solution. My own marriage had collapsed after nearly twenty-two years.

"Your wife got tired of playing second fiddle to your job on the police force." Tendrils of Pine-Sol crept around my head as Aidan spoke.

I know that, Aidan, but I still hate to admit that most of it was my fault.

Sarah continued, "Robin became jealous. Sammy plays guitar in a rock band at night and with his daytime job, she was feeling neglected. She was resentful of his time away from her. She even became suspicious that he was being intimate with the band's groupies.

"She became more and more insecure. She thought that he loved her less than his music and his Gibson guitar."

That Les Paul guitar was a gift that she and Charles had given to him at his high school graduation party. I remembered how excited Sammy had been when he'd unwrapped it.

The thoughts of my own divorce still weighed heavily on my mind. I understood what kinds of pressure that work and home could put on a person. The police department made demands on me after I was promoted to a detective and my wife began to feel isolated, thinking she had been squeezed out of my life. When she couldn't handle it anymore, we finally called it quits with our married life. I couldn't give her what she wanted and she couldn't live with my dedication to my career.

"At least she didn't string you along, Nephew. She felt it was time to move on and gave you a rest. Give her credit that she didn't continue to harp about your job," Aidan said. I thought I was in a lemon grove.

"Robin made up her mind to leave him, but not before she took his Les Paul guitar. She left a letter that was basically a ransom note. He tells me that the guitar is worth nearly thirteen thousand dollars. It's special because it's a Les Paul, whatever that means. Sammy can tell you more about it when you talk with him."

There has to more to this problem than just the guitar.

I sighed. Domestic cases were one of the most stressful problems that a cop had to face. A cop never knew what would happen responding to one of those calls.

The lemony Lysol smell eased a bit. *"She's your sister, Tommy. Are you going to turn her down?"* The sudden smell of chlorine bleach overpowered the lemon.

I'm going to do it, Aidan. There's no need for you to get upset and push me. I'm just reluctant to start. I'm not one hundred percent sure that I want to get between two quarreling lovers, especially when I'm related to one of them.

"I wouldn't ask, Tommy, but the loss of that guitar would be a major loss. He can't afford that kind of a financial set-back and to be truthful, we can't afford it either."

"All right, Sis, I'll need Sammy's phone number and address," I said.

"Thanks, big brother, you've always been there when I've needed you."

When she gave me the phone numbers and Sammy's address, she said, "Robin has probably gone back to her parent's home in Fox Chapel." Just before hanging up she said, "I love you, Tommy. You're a good brother."

"You're in for a rough one this time, I'm afraid," Aidan said as the fragrance of Pine-Sol eddied around my head replacing the harshness of the bleach. He could see something in my future.

When it's family, it's always a difficult situation. No one is ever satisfied. Someone somewhere is going to get their feelings hurt.

Before the scent of Pine-Sol disappeared, I heard Uncle LeClerc say, *"I hope that feelings are the only things that are going to get hurt."*

※

When I made the call to Sammy, I explained, "Your mom called. She wants me to help you get your guitar back."

I could tell that he was upset. He huffed, "I can handle this myself."

"I'm sure that you can, but a little help from a willing uncle can't hurt, can it?"

I heard a huge sigh. "She told me not to call the cops if I ever wanted to see my Les Paul in one piece again."

"I'm an EX-cop, remember?"

"Oh, ho, so now you're an EX-cop. Every other investigation we're on, you come on strong as being a Pittsburgh police officer, not one that's

retired," Uncle LeClerc said.

Give it a rest, Aidan. This is not the time.

I said to Sammy, "No arguments, I'm coming over. I'm sure that you have a photograph of your guitar. I'll need it."

"I have several, but the one that I like best is the one where Mom and Dad are giving it to me at graduation."

I found his apartment on a side street in Oakland. It was a walk up, located on the third floor. I was used to walking up two flights of stairs at my own place, but the third level of steps had me puffing hard. I wasn't accustomed to having to climb the extra floor.

I must be getting soft.

I stopped just outside of Sammy's door to catch my breath before knocking.

Inside, it was a typical young person's apartment. I could see a small living room, kitchenette, and a short hallway that probably led to a bedroom and bath. Posters lined the walls. Mismatched, hand-me-down furniture crowded the small sitting area.

"Have a seat, Uncle Tommy. Would you like a cup of coffee?"

"Sure."

I cringed when I saw him heating water in the microwave, then unscrew the top on a jar of a store brand instant coffee. The ding from the microwave summoned Sammy to the pull out the mug of hot water. I watched as he stirred in several heaping spoonsful of dark brown crystals. "I remember that you like you coffee hot, black, and strong."

Oh, joy.

"*Be nice,*" Aidan said. There was now a subtle, placating linen freshness to the room. "*He's trying his best.*"

I know someone who's going to get a coffee maker and several pounds of fresh ground coffee for Christmas this year. And wrote the reminder on a back page of my notebook.

I took a sip. The flavor wasn't as bad as instant used to be years ago, but it wasn't what I drank usually. The one time that I wished Uncle Aidan was there with his overpowering cleaning smells and he was nowhere to be found. Taking another sip from the mug, I sat it down on the small table beside me.

"Now, tell me about it." I already had my pad and pen out on the wide arm of the old chair. I placed them there while the "coffee" was being made. The springs from the seat of the chair poked at my seat from underneath the cushion. It wasn't as uncomfortable as my favorite stool at P's Café, but it was close.

"It all came to a head after I got a job as a warehouse worker at a local micro-brewery. I stack, move, and load the cases of beer as they come off the line. It doesn't make big bucks, but it pays the bills and I still have the time to practice my music before Robin comes home. I have about an hour and a half to play. She doesn't appreciate my music. She always complains about the 'noise.' I play back-up guitar and occasionally the keyboard. It depends on the song.

"Robin eventually told me she thought that I wasn't paying enough attention to her. Time after time, I've invited her to come with me to my gigs, but she refuses to go. At first, she liked the recognition of being known as a musician's girlfriend, but once she decided not to come along with me, she began to worry about the groupies. She was jealous of them, although I never, ever strayed."

"You can't play with your band now that she's taken your guitar?" I asked.

"Oh, no, I rarely play the Les Paul. It is too expensive. I keep it stored safely in its case at the back of my bedroom closet.

Robin knew where to hurt me the most when she walked off with my Les Paul. If she hadn't left a note when she took off, I might not have noticed that it was missing for months."

"Can I see the note?"

Sammy called over his shoulder as he headed down the hall, "I'm really worried about my guitar, Uncle Tommy. Robin left the G-string with the note."

"Leaving the G-string with the note would have really gotten his attention?" Aidan said with a chuckle, from the midst of a Lysol mist.

I don't understand why she would have left a pair of panties, Aidan. Why she would have left her G-string attached to the note? Why was Sammy worried so much that she had left it?

When Sammy came back, I understood what he meant and why LeClerc had laughed. The piece of wire was still taped to the letter. It was a string from his guitar. I took the note from him and told him to hold onto the wire.

The Lysol scent grew stronger. I could tell Aidan was looking over my shoulder. "That's one angry woman. Look at those pen strokes. They almost seem like slashes from a knife."

I agree. She's really angry.

I asked Sammy, "Are you sure that you didn't do something else to set her off?"

"She wanted to go on vacation to see her brother, but I said I couldn't go because of my new job and the gigs that I had lined up."

So much anger, there has to be more than just that. There has to be other incidents.

"Sammy, I can see the extreme anger in this note. Have you had issues with her before?"

"Uh...."

"Come clean with me, Sammy. If I don't know it all, I can't help you. Everything that you say is just between the two of us. It's confidential and I won't breathe a word to your parents."

Sammy plopped down on his old sofa across from me and put his hands over his face. It was a few minutes before he lifted his face and said, "Yeah, there's more."

"Yeah, what?"

"She gets mad, throws a fit, breaks things, and then she hits me. I've threatened to leave her and she just laughs. 'Just try it. I know where you live and I know your weaknesses.' Because I perform in public she would never hit me, punch me, or kick me where it would show."

"Why didn't you call…?"

"The police?" Sammy finished. He snorted, "She's into Mixed Martial Arts and she always has bruises. She said, 'If you call the cops, who do you think the police will believe, you or me?' She'd laugh and brush me off."

Lemon scented Clorox wafted into the room. *"She seems like one manipulative and evil-hearted woman."*

"She physically abused you? Did she leave any marks? Can you still see them?" I asked.

He nodded. "We had an argument when I was leaving for a gig the other night. She whipped up on me right before I went out the door. I was sore, but I had a contract to fulfill. By the time I got home, she'd packed her belongings, my guitar, and had gone."

"I'll need some photographs. I can use my cell phone for now, but we'll have to take better ones later." I wasn't going to tell him yet that I wanted another cop to get photographic evidence and to make out a report. It was the only way I could get an Emergency Protection Order.

He tugged off his long sleeved turtleneck. The bruises on his chest, under his arms, some over his kidneys, and on his back made me wince. There were bruises on his arms as well, where he had been grabbed and hit.

I snapped the pictures and then asked, "Is that it?"

He blushed, then stood up and dropped his sweatpants. Below his pair of plaid boxers, I could see several bruises on his right outer thigh and a huge one on his inner left thigh. As I focused the camera on the inner thigh injury, Sammy said, "She almost got me to sing soprano, but I moved. If she would have gotten the family jewels I might not have been able to play with the band. I think that's what she intended and would have tried to kick me again if I hadn't fallen to the floor, faking that she'd been right on target. I rolled on the floor holding myself for several minutes before she walked away."

After standing there awkwardly for a few seconds, Sammy saw me glance at his furniture. He bent over, then pulled up his pants. He said, "We had better furniture, but she would get upset and vandalize something. I refused to buy more just to have her break it and she refused to approach her parents to buy more. They have money and have never refused to get anything for her."

"I'll need her full name, birth date, and her parent's address and a photograph of your guitar."

As I copied the information in my notebook, he hurried down the hallway.

He returned from the bedroom with the photo. It was of him in his cap and gown. He and Sarah were posing with the Les Paul guitar. There was a large red bow fastened to its neck. A huge smile covered his face.

Taking the photograph, I beat a hasty retreat before Sammy could decide to re-warm my coffee, or offer to make another cup for me.

Pausing at the door, I said, "If she contacts you in any way—a visit, a call, an e-mail, a text, or a carrier pigeon—you need to notify me right away." I handed him one of my cards after writing my cell phone number on the back of it.

"Thanks, Uncle Tommy, but what's a carrier pigeon?"

"Google it," I called as I jogged down the three flights of steps. I had to hurry if I wanted to catch the bus to the police station. The next thing I wanted to do was a background check on Robin before deciding on which course I wanted to take.

※

"Hey, Sarge." Sergeant Duggan was at the desk when I walked in.

"Tommy, I've been seeing more of you since you've retired than when you actually put in time here," he joked.

"Ain't that the truth? I've been trying to do some writing and people keep dumping more cases in my lap for me to solve. It does, at times, seem that there are more crimes for me now than I had when I worked here."

"What brings you in today, you old warhorse?" Sarge paused, then said, "I figure you're here because you need my help… again."

"You're right, Sarge. I need you to do a background check on a person who's displaying a violent streak to one of my family members," I said.

"An abuse case?" Sarge said as he raised his eyebrows.

When I nodded, he said, "I can do that search for you here on my computer, Tommy."

"Her name is Robin Naist." I gave him her birth date and addresses of her parents and of Sammy's apartment.

"H-m-m-m. M-m-m. M-m-m," Sarge hummed as he made the search. "I see she's had several incidents as a juvie, but those are sealed. You'd have to get a court order to open them. But, since then, there were two occasions that the police were called and reports were made. She assaulted her own mother eighteen months ago and the other call about three weeks ago was for an assault on a bouncer who tried to escort her out of a bar. He asked her to leave and she beat him up. Paramedics took him to the hospital for stitches and a broken wrist." He paused, looked at me over the top of his reading glasses, then said, "She beat up a bouncer?"

"Yeah, she's a Mixed Martial Arts expert," I explained.

There was a sharp chlorine odor that filled my nostrils. *"This is going to be a hard one for sure."*

Sarge whistled, then said, "Tommy, you're gonna need to watch this one closely if you want to stay healthy."

"Don't I know it."

Sarge turned the monitor to where I could read the information from the bar fight. The chlorine eased and Uncle LeClerc said, *"You'll need to talk to the bartender of DiMichael's Bar& Grill."*

I know that, Aidan. I want to talk to as many people who were there that night, especially the bouncer.

I wrote down the names. That was part of my plan for later.

※

I flagged down a taxi. I wanted to check out Robin's parent's home in Fox Chapel and riding a bus wasn't an option. The two-story house was built of cut stone with a wide, precisely manicured lawn. An unobtrusive driveway disappeared in a long curve behind the house. I asked the cabby to wait as I did a quick cursory survey of the grounds. The drive ended at a carriage house. Robin's white Audi was parked outside the back door. Everything was neat and spoke of money. I returned to the cab before I could be spotted and headed back to my apartment.

I'd butted heads with violent criminals before, and I didn't like the idea of tackling this case and this woman without the backing of the police department. This gal was had a wealthy father and that made a confrontation with Robin and her family so much worse.

"Money has a way of speaking loudly here in Pittsburgh," LeClerc said. "I've seen it."

It's like that in every city, Uncle Aidan.

The scent of Pine-Sol drifted back at me. "It will be very hard to pull this one together. You'll have to plan each step carefully if you want to stay healthy, help Sammy get his guitar back in one piece, and settle the score," LeClerc said.

I don't know about settling the score, but I still have friends on the force. I'm hoping I can get them to help. Uncle Aidan, if you were better at relaying clues, I could see what's ahead sooner and plan better, but you were never too free with sharing them with me.

"What do you want me to say to you? 'Don't fret' or 'that she's stringing him along' or 'that she's trying to get him to dance to another tune,' but those won't help you at all." The scent of Pine-Sol intensified, then just as suddenly, the smell disappeared. Aidan had gone.

I hoped that he left to look for clues, but knowing Uncle Aidan, I had just made him angry and he went somewhere to sulk.

I called the station house to see if Dave and Marty were free to take some photos of Sammy's injuries and to take his statement. "Hey, guys, I have a favor to ask."

They said they were tied up with another case, but they'd send someone out. I made quick call to be sure that Sammy was going to be home and I invited myself over, telling Sammy I'd be there in about an hour.

I stopped at a deli for a large cup of coffee to go before I made the long climb up the stairs to his apartment. I wasn't sure that I could handle another cup of instant.

A smell of lemon Pine-Sol drifted into the stairwell. "*I don't think that Sammy will like what you're planning.*" Aidan had returned.

It may be a surprise for Sammy, but I had to get the police involved to get an Emergency Protection Order. I had to arrange legal protection for him from Robin. The cops could issue it when they arrived and saw his bruises.

I also wanted to have official photographic evidence and a police report filed, so Sammy and I could arrange for a Protection from Abuse Order to be issued by the court. I knocked, "Sammy, it's your uncle Tommy. Open up."

There was a delay, but when he opened the door, I noticed a lamp had been knocked over and broken.

"She came back," I said to him. It was a statement and not a question.

Sammy nodded.

"Why didn't you call?"

"She just left, Uncle. I didn't have time." He held up something small silver and white. "She threw one of the keys to my guitar into my face before she left. She's going to destroy my Les Paul," he whined. "She's giving it back to me one piece at a time."

"I have a couple of guys from the police department coming over in a bit. I need to have them take photographs of your injuries and file a report so that I can get an Emergency Protection Order issued to keep her away and to keep you safe.

"Next, we are getting a locksmith to come over and change all of your locks. It might not be legal, but I want to be able to sleep at night and not have to worry about her coming over and killing you some time."

"She wouldn't kill me. She loves me."

"When your aunt and I separated after twenty-three years of marriage, there was more love between us than what I see here."

The fragrance of the Pine-Sol had intensified. *"If this is love, I'd be afraid to see hate."*

I couldn't agree more with you, Aidan.

A knock on the door interrupted my thoughts.

When Sammy opened the door, it was Duffy McCune and a cop I'd never seen before named Willis DuVane.

"Hey, Duffy, they got you breaking in the new guys?" Duffy had been a partner with me on the force for several years.

"Tommy, what are you doing here?"

"This is my nephew, Sammy, and I'm doing my best to see he's not the next homicide victim for the department."

I quickly explained the situation. Willis jogged back to the car for the camera. I knew they would need pictures and I had Sammy peel down to a pair of gym shorts to pose for the photos.

Duffy said, "Whew, it looks like somebody really had it in for you. They must have thought that you were a punching bag."

"It wasn't a *they*; it was only one person. When you two are done with the pictures, I need an E. P.O. for my nephew. I can't have his girlfriend assaulting him again. She's a Mixed Martial Artist."

Sammy blushed with the mention he'd been unable to protect himself from a girl.

Being the professional that he was, Duffy didn't make a remark about being attacked by a woman. "It's as good as done."

Willis and Duffy left the apartment with the photos and the report. They were gone and Sammy had his Emergency Protection Order in hand.

"We'll get a restraining order Sammy, probably tomorrow."

"I can't, Uncle. I have to work."

"Let me work on that. I'll try to catch a judge for lunch time. You can tell your boss that you'll need an hour or so to handle a legal matter. I'll let you know as soon as I can arrange a time."

Sammy gave a huge sigh.

"What?" I asked.

"I wish you hadn't done this," Sammy said. "It's only going to make her more upset."

"I need to legally create some distance between the two of you. You don't need to suffer any more abuse"

He looked at me with pleading eyes. "At least don't tell my mom. I don't want her to know that she was right and I can't take care of myself."

In seconds, a swirl of bleach swept in. Aidan said, *"This young man's in way over his head. He can't take care of himself. If he really didn't want his mom to know, how did his mother find out that his guitar was missing?"*

So, I asked, "How did your mom find out that your guitar was missing?"

"I was so upset when I found that it was gone, without thinking, I called my mom. I was at a loss of what to do. I didn't tell her any of the other things that happened to me. I was too embarrassed."

More or Les

※

I stopped at P's Café for a late lunch. I needed a shot of joe to keep me going. Claiming my usual seat at the counter, I settled in. Without asking, Vera slid my usual cup of coffee in front of me.

"What else can I get for you, Tommy?"

"A less stressful life," I joked. Picking up my cup, I sipped the scalding, black liquid. "Just gimme your special."

A knife, fork, and spoon wrapped in a paper napkin appeared out of nowhere. A few minutes later, she placed a plate of liver and onions with a pile of mashed potatoes and green beans under my nose. "I love liver'n onions, but haven't had 'em in quite awhile."

Vera leaned on her elbows and said, "You know, if you need me to do anything, just call me." I noticed that her tops weren't as low cut since she married.

"I know, Vera. Thanks."

As I ate, I contemplated my next move.

A soft smell of fresh linen filled my nostrils. *Yes, Uncle Aidan, what do you want?*

"*You need to finish your meal. It's time to hit the bar. It may be a little bit early, but there's no time for you to rest yet,*" Aidan said.

I'm not like you. I need to eat once and awhile. Give me some time. The bar's not going to move or be shut down by the time I finish my meal. Let me enjoy my food and take your Lysol with you. I wiggled my butt on the Naugahyde covered stool, trying to relax and drink my refill of coffee while it was still hot. The stool didn't get any more comfortable, but just to prove my point, I took my time eating. When I couldn't delay any longer, I paid my bill and headed off to DiMichael's Bar & Grill.

It was still a bit early, but I knew the barkeep would be in, getting the bar set up for the night's customers.

DiMichael's was a dive. It was a hangout for college kids and young people. They chose the bar not for the atmosphere or the music, but because management was less than scrupulous about closely examining their I.D.s.

I walked inside the long, dark room. A stool lined bar covered one side, several small tables claimed the other. At the far end was a pool table and a juke box. Most of the light came from the advertisements for beer hanging behind the bar and the light that hunched over the pool table.

My eyes hadn't adjusted yet when from the darkness a male voice hoarse from years of inhaling cigarette smoke asked, "What can I get you?"

"A draft beer and some information." I never drink, but to grease the wheels, I bought something.

He pushed the glass of amber liquid in front of me. "Are you a cop?"

"Not any more. I'm retired, but I still need to find out what went on with the girl who whipped up your bouncer."

"Oh, her. I'll be more than glad to tell you about her. Her old man smoothed things over. He came in and paid for the damages and the hospital bills for Jerome."

"Jerome?"

"My bouncer. She was a holy terror. Jerome is six foot three and two hundred and forty-five pounds. Most of it is muscle. She demolished him, kicking and punching. He was off for three weeks because of his injuries. I think he's losing his nerve. I may soon have to look for a replacement."

"What happened that night?"

"She was getting loud and disruptive. I nodded at Jerome.

He walked over to her and asked her to settle down or leave. When she refused to do either, he placed his hand on her elbow to direct her out. It was though he lit the fuse on a stick of dynamite. She exploded in a flurry of punches and kicks.

"She was still wound up when the cops arrived. The two who responded couldn't get close until two more uniforms arrived. Then they had to empty a full can of pepper spray in her face before they could cuff her and drag her out. Jerome was still on the floor."

While we were talking, Jerome walked in. The cast on his arm almost glowed against his dark cocoa skin.

The bartender called, "Hey, Jerome. This guy's here about the woman who whooped your ass."

"That bitch! What does she want?" Jerome growled.

"I want to know what happened. I have a client who is being assaulted by her and I am trying to prevent any more trouble for him."

After he recalled the same story almost word for word as the man behind the bar, he said, "He tried to buy me off with a couple of bucks. I refused. Then her old man hired a lawyer who made the judge believe that his daughter thought I was accosting her and that I was going to hurt her," he laughed . "Me, hurt her? You can see what she did to me." He lifted his cast for me to see, pointing to the healing scar on his forehead.

He wouldn't say anything else, but he did say, "I'm praying that girl gets what's coming to her."

When I left, unease plagued my mind. I hated to think about the inevitable confrontation with her.

※

I called Sammy. "I just spoke with Judge Harris and he's making time to meet you and me in his chambers at lunch time today. I need you to bring the E. P. O. with you. I'll pick up a copy of the police report and copies of the photographs."

At the courthouse, we met in the judge's chamber. After reading the information in Duffy's report and seeing the pictures, he had no problem signing the Protection from Abuse Order. I don't think he recognized Robin's name or associated her name with her father's. Robin's dad liked to throw his weight around in city hall on occasion. Judge Harris had little to worry about. He was safe for the next four years. He'd just been re-elected.

Sammy and I left the judge's chamber. I told him, "If she contacts you in any way, call me. Don't respond to her for any reason. You need to notify me immediately. We need to work together to get your Les Paul back, safe and sound."

※

The next day I got a call from Sammy. "Uncle, I just got a text from Robin. She apologized and said that she was sorry. She said she'll bring my guitar back if she can move in with me again. She wants me to sign a paper saying that she hadn't harmed my guitar. She finished by saying that she loves me."

"Listen to me, Sammy. Don't text her. Don't call her. Don't send her an e-mail, facebook, or anything at all. I have a few things to do, and then I'll come over to your place to get the ball rolling. I don't want you to do a blessed thing."

It was time for me to actually figure out the logistics.

I caught the aroma of liniment oil.

Funny, Uncle Aidan, very funny.

"If Robin chooses to fight, someone might get hurt and one

of those some ones might be you, one of your friends, or might even be me," I said before I hung up.

I decided to set up a meeting. It needed it to be in a public place, but not an area that would be congested or busy where an innocent bystander might interfere or get hurt. The cop part of me said I needed to protect them. I didn't have too much time to decide before Robin got antsy.

"*Near a police station, too?*" LeClerc's voice cut through my thoughts and a lemony Pine-Sol scent covered the liniment smell. "*It would be nice to have the cavalry close at hand in case the meeting heads south. Maybe a small park area or an open city lot.*"

I remembered that there was a small sitting park just around the corner from the police station. It was little more than a few benches, several planters, and a couple of trees. It would be out of the way and perfect.

※

It was Saturday. Sammy only worked for half a day on Saturdays. He'd be finished with his job and be home. It was too early for him to be out on a gig with his band, but I called ahead anyway. He was waiting for me when I arrived. A steaming mug of the same instant coffee was also waiting for me. I swallowed my pride much more easily than I was able to choke down that cup of imitation coffee.

Setting the mug aside, I said, "Gimme your cell." I looked at the text. It was exactly as Sammy had told me. Robin wanted move back into his apartment and into his life. I texted her on Sammy's cell, that way he hadn't actually violated the restraining order. "Willing to meet. Consent to terms once I see the guitar is safe and in one piece." I gave her the address for the meeting and the time of five p.m.

She texted back the message, "Five thirty. Don't be late." Even when she wasn't close to Sammy, she had to try to be in control.

I had no sooner left Sammy's apartment and made it down to the street level when he called me, "Uncle Tommy, Robin just called. She must have borrowed another person's phone. I didn't recognize the number. When I answered, she began to scream. 'I'll send that precious guitar back to you in pieces. Small pieces where it was never meant to come apart and not just a string or a key.' I had to wait for her tirade to settle before I could say anything."

Apparently, the sheriff had found her and delivered the restraining order.

Sammy continued, "I told her, it wasn't me. My mom called my uncle and he had a judge friend who sent out the restraining order when my uncle saw that you beat me.

"Then she screamed, 'Who does your uncle think he is? I'm so upset. I want to punch or break something. It insults me that a sheriff came to my mom and dad's house and parked his car out front. Can you imagine what the neighbors are thinking? Just you wait until my dad finds out who your uncle is. He'll be sorrier than you're gonna be, if you don't get rid of that restraining order and fast. You should be happy that I'm not where I have the guitar hidden right now.

"'I'll still meet you at 5:30 and you better be ready to reconcile and sign away that order.'

"She hung up before I could say anything more and I called you."

Lysol assaulted my nostrils. *"The cat's out of the bag and that cat has her claws out for sure. She is going to be after you and Sammy,"* Aidan said.

You're right, Uncle Aidan. I know about her and her dad's type. He's going to be looking for pay back, too. He has money and likes to show it. He wields his wealth and power like a battering ram. It couldn't be helped. We had to have the restraining order to keep Sammy safe.

※

Sergeant Duggan called. "Tommy boy, you really kicked over an ant hill."

"What's happening down there?"

"Robert Naist came down to the station, throwing a fit as well as a chair. He cornered Duffy and Willis about their investigation of his daughter's assault on your nephew. Somehow he managed to get a copy of the report. He had Duffy and Willis's name as the investigating officers and has your name listed as a witness. After creating a scene, he stormed out of here breathing Hellfire and brimstone."

A burst of Pine-Sol hit me full in the face. *"You'll really have to watch your back now, Tommy. There are two of them. He'd break your neck if he had a chance and Robin would beat you to a pulp as quickly as she did on Sammy,"* Aidan warned.

Sarge said, "He is out for blood. He acted as though the sheriff delivering the Protection from Abuse papers was an unforgivable insult. He's not going to quickly forget this."

"Thanks for the heads up, Sarge." A bead of sweat trickled down the back of my collar.

※

It was almost five thirty p.m. and everything was in place. It would now be a waiting game. Duffy and Willis were nearby at a street vendor's cart buying a hot dog and keeping a sharp eye out for Robin. Sammy was pacing nervously on the sidewalk and I was sitting on one of the benches, reading a newspaper and sipping on a cup of *real* black coffee.

I almost missed seeing Robin when she arrived. She drove up as the passenger in a shiny black Mercedes Benz. She threw open the door. A horn blared as she rushed across the street, dodging the traffic. She hurried to Sammy and shoved a paper under his nose. "Sign it. Sign it now, you little worm." The acid in her voice fairly dripped from her lips. Standing directly in front of him, she shook with barely restrained anger.

Before it could escalate, Duffy and Willis moved in. She had ignored the restraining order and now could be removed by the authorities. I saw Willis using his radio to call for back up. About to confront Robin, they wanted to have reserves on hand in case they were needed.

So that there would be no confusion, Duffy called out after showing his badge. "Police, Robin, stop. You're under arrest. Put your hands on top of your head."

Uncle Aidan said as he appeared, camouflaged in a cloud of chlorine bleach, *"She's not going to surrender. She's going to fight."*

Sure enough, she spun around and took an attack position, allowing the paper she carried to flutter to the ground. I heard Duffy call, "Watch yourself, Willis." Then to Robin, "Police, you're under arrest. You need to surrender before you get hurt."

If the situation hadn't been so dangerous, I would have laughed. If anyone had to be careful not to get hurt, it would be Duffy.

She prepared herself to do bodily harm to anyone who dared to come close enough to her.

Dropping my newspaper, I grabbed Sammy and pulled him out of the danger area. I didn't want him to get hurt in any of the inevitable fray. Pushing him to safety behind a concrete bench, I ordered, "Stay there."

Robin took a swing at Duffy. He was able to avoid it because he hadn't allowed himself to come within her reach, and as a cop, he was a veteran of quite a few attacks.

That's all that it took to get the brouhaha started. While Robin's attention was focused on Duffy, Willis swung up his can of pepper spray and hit her full in the face with a long, forceful stream.

Robin threw her hands to her face and eyes. Between the gagging spells, the language that she spewed was unbefitting anyone, let alone a woman. Even though she was temporarily blinded, she started to flail one arm around. Willis caught it and snapped the hand cuff tight. Duffy pried the other from her face and bent it behind her back, forcing her to the ground. Between them both, they managed to finally secure her with the cuffs. She still tried to kick. Willis and Duffy had to sit on her to keep her from hurting herself or them.

"Hold still and we'll get some water to wash off some of the spray out of your eyes," Willis said.

Robin paid no attention and still thrashed about on the sidewalk, cursing.

The odor of the pepper spray drifted my way. It covered Aidan's usual odor of cleaning supplies and I didn't recognize that he was visiting until he said, *"It's not over yet."*

And it wasn't. Although she was handcuffed and held down, her dad was not.

Squealing brakes caused me to look across the street. The driver's door of the Mercedes had been thrown open. Robert Naist hurled himself out of the car and into traffic. He rushed across the street. I could only assume that he was about to interfere with a policeman in his line of duty. I hopped over the bench to intercept the human missile.

He had almost reached Duffy. He was swearing and calling the cops names in a language only decipherable by an old sailor. "Let go of my daughter," were the only words repeatable.

As soon as my body blocked Robert's sight of his daughter, we hit the concrete in a tangle of arms and legs. The knee on my Chinos ripped. By that time, Duffy and Willis had Robin under control and the boys in uniform arrived. They jumped on top of Robert Naist and me, trying to separate us. Every time I thought I was free, Robert would grab and punch me.

Finally, Robert was pulled off of me. We'd been separated by the uniforms, but he wasn't finished. He was still intent on rescuing Robin. Breaking free, he headed toward Willis with balled fists. One of the uniformed patrolmen pulled his Taser and shot Robert in the back. The prongs had hit their target. *Z-z-z-z-ap.*

When the 50,000 volt charge coursed through him, his whole body stiffened. He dropped to the pavement, shaking and crying. "No more. No more! I quit. Stop. No more." He was cuffed.

Paramedics arrived several minutes later to attend to Robin's eyes, to remove the Taser prongs from Robert's torso, and to clean the scrape on my knee.

Oh, man, look at that. I put my finger through the rip in my knee. *There's a hole in my pants. If I'd have been still working, I might have gotten reimbursed for them. But now, they're ruined. And look at my brogans, they're all scuffed up.*

The stench of pepper spray was still strong. I only knew Uncle LeClerc was there when I heard him say, *"You can always cut off the pant legs and make a pair of walking shorts."*

What? These legs haven't seen the light of day since I was a kid, playing in our front yard with my brother, Johnny. These pants are a total loss.

"Maybe Mr. Naist will pay for a new pair. After all, he owes you. You prevented him from assaulting a police officer."

Oh, no, Aidan. That's one thing I learned not to do. I won't try to beard a lion.

Both he and his daughter were booked.

"I wonder what his lawyer is going to say about this. Maybe it will help to settle the score for a lot of people," Aidan said.

In all of the excitement, I'd lost track of Sammy. Looking around, I saw him standing near the opened back door of the Mercedes. His red Les Paul guitar was cradled in his arms. I saw him mouthing, "Thank you, Uncle Tommy." That was worth more than a pair of Chinos and scuffed pair of shoes any day.

About the Author

A father, grandfather, and nursing supervisor, Thomas Beck has lived in Southwest Pennsylvania his entire life, except for a stint as a naval corpsman. Writing from his home in the mountains near Acme, he draws on past experiences and creative thoughts to weave together baskets of tales for the reader.

Made in the USA
Charleston, SC
13 November 2016